The Sum of Her

The Scent of Her

Kathleen Hewitt

eLectio Publishing

Little Elm, TX

www.eLectioPublishing.com

The Scent of Her

By Kathleen Hewitt

Copyright © 2013 by Kathleen Hewitt

Cover Copyright © 2013 by Abbey Newkirk

Author Photograph by Lucy Wightman

ISBN: 0615916805

ISBN-13: 978-0615916804

Published by eLectio Publishing, Little Elm, TX

www.eLectioPublishing.com

For my children,

Matthew, Andrew and Kathryn

With enduring love.

TABLE OF CONTENTS

INTRODUCTION 1
CHAPTER 1 5
CHAPTER 2 9
CHAPTER 3 15
CHAPTER 4 21
CHAPTER 5 27
CHAPTER 6 35
CHAPTER 7 45
CHAPTER 8 51
CHAPTER 9 57
CHAPTER 10 61
CHAPTER 11 65
CHAPTER 12 71
CHAPTER 13 77
CHAPTER 14 83
CHAPTER 15 89
CHAPTER 16 93
CHAPTER 17 105
CHAPTER 18 109
CHAPTER 19 115
CHAPTER 20 121
CHAPTER 21 123
ACKNOWLEDGMENTS 127

"And in my hour of darkness, Mother Mary comes to me, speaking words of wisdom, let it be."

John Lennon and Paul McCartney

INTRODUCTION

Hers was a silent kitchen. A cheap ticking clock hung from a nail; always ten minutes behind—something to count on. The cold chrome table on shaky legs was still wedged against the wall, as though to make room. Torn red vinyl-covered stools offered seating, but never enough for every O'Callaghan at once. This was no gathering place. It was a hollow, expressionless room then and now.

See through rayon curtains, a price tag still on one, hung over the sink, and no smells lingered in the air of meals lovingly prepared. The roasting pans stayed buried under the stove. The only oven mitt was hardly worn but scorched. I had been grateful for the attempt, that once, for the Christmas cookies shaped like bells. I had wanted to sprinkle the red sugar on them but they were left in too long. She had forgotten about them. Lonely walls stood cracked, without sentiment. The dull beige paint cried for hooks from which an apron or a sweater could be grabbed on the fly or for a homey cross-stitch to remind us that the cook was in charge. But there was only the kitchen Madonna, chipped and faded and long stowed in a corner behind the empty rusted canister. Neglect was the only dish on the menu and there was plenty of that to go around.

I stood in my mother's kitchen years after the emptiness of my childhood on this June morning. She'd died the month before, right after Mother's Day. I needed to gather what was left and close things up. I opened the window hoping for a breeze, keeping it from slamming down with an old wooden ruler.

I had taken to wearing flip flops everyday and that morning the dented aluminum door scraped the back of my ankle, spilling fresh blood all over the hem of my jeans. I swiped at the stinging gash with my finger. I stepped into my life of thirty years ago with a fresh wound. I told myself it was better to feel, even if all I felt was pain.

    I ran my hands along the countertop still sticky with resin from a life of red hard boxed Marlboros. I tugged at the junk drawer and it stuck on the left as it had done forever. I yanked it open to find reminders and successes that I hoped would adorn the refrigerator door. Not like most peoples' drawers full of pens, bits of string, notepads...all the just-in-case stuff. This drawer was nothing more than a half-hearted attempt to hold all things considered unnecessary and unwanted. I nudged around a few old papers. That permission slip for a field trip I couldn't go on sat glaring at me. I was the only kid in class who couldn't go and I watched everyone get on the bus while I sat alone in the classroom. Ancient spelling tests of mine surfaced with 100% in the corners and comments like, "Keep up the great work, Kate!" Coffee stains covered the 'i' before 'e' except after 'c' words on one. I studied so hard. I got A's in all my classes, except for math. Huge shiny red stars wrinkled and stained had me swallowing hard but seeing the brush and the elastic took my breath away. I put it there for a morning when my mother might help comb out my long curly wild hair. Maybe she could make it smooth and shiny so I could wear a long, swinging ponytail. This drawer I now emptied of forgotten expectations that were stashed out of sight, out of mind, pushed aside without a thought. I pulled my long hair back in that elastic and started to fill, hardly fill, a giant green trash bag, with a few little girl hopes.

    I moved to the table, careful not to trip over the green mottled linoleum floor, worn and uneven. My father had put it down himself to save money and tacked the cap of a beer bottle under a square. It stayed there. He tried, I know, it took a whole weekend and he had to work come Monday but when things were broken in our house, they just didn't get fixed.

My childhood kitchen had not been a place of birthday cupcakes or tollhouse anything. The floor had never known the mess of flour or spilled batter. The peeling yellowing cabinets held more deviled ham than anyone should ever eat. I had eaten it every day—it was that or go hungry—even when the kids at school called it pigs' tongues. And I'd been hungry all the time...hungry for so much.

My ankle had stopped bleeding, but was sore. The gash was swelling already and the kitchen still didn't recognize me. It held nothing of the girl I was and yet it held everything for me. The clock hands were at 4:00. I reached up to lift it off the nail and plaster came with it. My eyes were gritty with dust as I added the timeless treasure to the trash bag along with the jar of yellow mustard from the moldy fridge. A few Flintstone glasses and some plastic forks and that would be it. The yard sale had taken care of the rest. A big "free" sign was all it took. The house would belong to another family in just a week. I held the Madonna and prayed that this new family would know the way Swiss dot curtains could dance at the window. I prayed for a hearty beef stew and crusty bread to be passed around a steady table. Maybe the baby of the family would run to the arms of the oldest and sit on a lap, lost in good, filling food. A rushing sound filled my ears and I leaned back into the cool wall. I struggled to focus, my eyes blurry with tears. I took it all in one last time. Silently I thanked the wall for its' steadying comfort while the kitchen stared back at me, bold with indifference. If kitchens talked, this one would say there's no one home. I shut the window on the breeze that never came. Madonna tucked under my arm, I closed the door for the very last time.

CHAPTER 1

The story of my mother and me clings to my shoulders like a too-tight turtleneck. I keep yanking at the collar, trying to stretch the fabric, but wearing it anyway without the give. The hardest thing is in the telling. After all, it is only one daughter's experience. It's personal, maybe just ordinary. It could have been worse; it has been for some. Irish whispers, the lace-curtain kind of Boston, ask me to bury it. They repeat, in characteristic, quiet tones that I need to put it away, like a hand me down silky kerchief pushed to the back of a cedar chest, near the white gloves. The hope chest that held my mother's wedding gown also held things for rain, wind and funerals. It was also full of things to wear on St. Patrick's Day. A day that was also whispered about, "those damn drinking Irish." Heartache is a deep bureau of its' own. You can close the drawers but you know what's inside. There's only so much you can make room for. Lock the door and hide the key but the banging continues. This story won't let me go. Trying to wrench free from its' hold, I am a freckled faced toddler fighting the grip of a steadying mother. The pages are written on my soul, clutching me with a force both loving and unyielding. Words wake me from a safe womb of silence, living out loud with a life of their own. There are limits to what we can hide from. There are limits, I insist, to what we can hold on to. I will free my tale, my solid companion and pray that it all sets me free, too.

There is a love we don't talk about. A love between a mother and her daughter, a love that keeps you standing close to her, feeling the hairs on her arms, and willing her to reach for you. I'd do handstands and cartwheels, wanting to draw her near, and my wet hope-filled eyes begged, "Please, Mama, look at me, in all my glory!" Spreading her 'Pucker Up' lipstick on my mouth and pressing her Coty powder into my cheeks might bring an indulgent smile. On a good day, we might color together or cuddle up with a Beatrix Potter book. Moments of connection promised more of the same. The craving for more is as palpable and constant as breathing in and out, for me, anyway. The longing is a dress I wear and never take off. In the remembering of a little girl's heart, it seems like a dream, all the brief moments lined up in a row. And the wish for more lasts a lifetime.

Other children luxuriously watched cartoons; I watched my mother. In the trance of girlhood, our lives unraveled, every day a little bit more. I was the curly-haired girl with the blushing cheeks, mouth wrapped around a huge sour pickle from the corner store. My feet dangling from the kitchen stool, Pixie Sticks in hand, I waited for my mother to wake up. My sugar coated lips grinned with anticipation. So very patient, the loyal puppy, I greeted her every day as though she were the most important person in the world, because she was.

She brushed by me in her nightgown. "Good Morning, Morning Glory!" I said. Instead of answering, she reached for her coffee mug. I pretended I heard, "Good Morning, Morning Sunshine!" instead of the quiet that met me. I closed my eyes and imagined that she ruffled my hair and kissed the tip of my nose, a nose just like hers.

Then I watched her slip away, admiring her walk. I could smell the sheets that hadn't been changed in a while and a tiny bit of violet powder as she passed. My dad said that Mom had a wiggle, whatever that was. I knew it was a good thing, though, so I practiced her sashaying step after she had gone back upstairs. Sweet and very sour love filled me. I licked the sugar from my lips, washed my fingers and ran as fast as I could to the bus. I'd run home too, to be sure she was still there. Sitting on the bus, in the only seat left, my heart was so full that my eyes burned. Love hurts sometimes and that's a bittersweet truth. She had wanted me. She told me this herself when she dragged me to St. Helen's church, one block over. She roughly tied a kerchief about my head and she bobby pinned a black lacy mantilla on her head before we went in. My wrist hurt, she was holding it so hard and we knelt at the altar in front of Jesus. She made the sign of the cross and she was whispering words that I couldn't understand so I said the Glory Be, the shortest prayer that I knew. "Kate," she said, "When your father and I got married, we went to New York City on our honeymoon. Do you know what a honeymoon is?" I shook my head, kind of not wanting to know because she was frightening me somehow. She went on, "people used to say that you must have been born exactly nine months after our honeymoon, exactly on our honeymoon night. They make it sound impossible, that maybe your father and I did something wrong. Do you know what I mean?" "No, Momma, I really don't, but it's ok." "No! It's not ok", she said, "I went to Saint Patrick's Cathedral and I prayed at every single altar, there are over fifty altars there, Kate. I prayed on my knees with my eyes closed at the feet of every saint, Jesus and the Blessed Mother, that you would be conceived that night, that very night." She tightly tugged at my wrist, "Do you understand, Kate, do you now"? "My prayers were answered that day, God heard me. He gave me you. If you pray hard enough, God will always hear you. Don't ever forget to pray, ever. Ever." My mother's eyes demanded this from me and I would not let her down, especially now that I knew she had really wanted me.

CHAPTER 2

Kneeling on the worn hardwood floors in my room, I prayed. "Dear Jesus and Mary and any saints that are listening, please make me a good girl. Please keep my mother happy enough to stay. Amen."

  I got up and dressed for school, grabbled a fistful of Fruit Loops and went back upstairs to say goodbye to my mother before I left. That morning I was to be in a play, *Sara Crew*, and I had the lead. The quietest girl in the world was Sara Crew on a stage at the Gridley Bryant elementary school. I wanted to remind Mom that the show started at 11:30 a.m. and if she sat on the left she'd see me better. I had to sit six inches from the maroon velvet curtain and eat a whole package of Parker Dinner rolls. Sara Crew was a poor girl on her own and she had to eat the food as though she'd never eat again.

  I leaned against the bedroom door and watched my mother put on her favorite dress. It was sleeveless and covered in roses; red and dark pink blooms that melted and bled into each other. She smelled like the air after a sultry, humid downpour. Away from her I closed my eyes and became the fragrant emptiness. It was my perfume of familiarity; it held me and calmed me as nothing else did. "Mom, you look soooo pretty today. I asked Mrs. Thompson to give you a ride, so don't worry about a thing. She'll show you which door to go in. She's always at the school. Wish me luck!"

  My mother never made it to my big performance. I got a standing ovation and the popular kids started talking to me. Glad I had the dinner rolls because I had forgotten to make my lunch that day and I wasn't going to get into that free lunch line.

  On the days I had to be in school I was impatient to get home. I knew anything could happen when you were gone that long. As if I had special powers, I sent my mother messages with my thoughts as I sat through math and science and English. *I'll be home soon, Mom. Don't go anywhere.* I ran from the bus to the back door, whispering *please, please, please, please*, over and over. If I said it enough times everything would be okay. I raced into the kitchen, the tightly wound spring on the door catching at the back of my sneaker. I instinctively knew when she was gone, felt the stillness in the air and a new wound. One rainy spring day, I found her rose dress in her closet under a month's worth of soiled clothes. It seemed that it was always at the end of winter that she would leave even though I told her over and over just how soon spring would come. I sat on the floor and clutched it to my chest, burrowing my nose into the musky fabric. Her dress was the only thing I had to hold onto, her spirit captured in my small hands.

When Mom wore her rose dress, things were all right. When she went away I crossed out each passing day on the calendar, counting and praying, until she came home. I hung her dress in my closet, pushed my things aside to make room. I sprayed her perfume on my fingertips and ran them along the neckline and then on my wrists.

On a rare and perfect day just before Easter, Dad dropped my mother and me off in Quincy Square. She helped me choose a lime green dress in the latest style and fishnet stockings the color of a Creamsicle. Then she took me to see Clarisse at the beauty parlor to have my hair cut and styled. Clarisse teased it and sprayed it. It looked like the huge cotton candy that I'd get at the Marshfield Fair and if I touched it, I'd stick to it. I felt too young for such a coiffure and thought I looked stupid, but my mother said I looked like a model. I snuck glances at myself in the store windows the rest of the afternoon, secretly hoping that she was right. She was exhausted when we got home that day and slept on the couch until it was time for me to go to bed. I whispered, "Thanks, Mom, it was so much fun." "Mom, mom?" I thought she didn't hear me. She finally mumbled something about wearing a hairnet to bed. I found one and I pulled it on.

On my bed, I laid propped on elbows going over every detail of the day, smiling, with my legs moving to an Easter parade song on my transistor radio. While Mom slept, I had magical thoughts about the next time we'd enjoy such a day. My hair, full of Aqua Net, was all ready for Easter, a week ahead of time. I loved her so much. I stared at her closed bedroom door and I daydreamed that Mom would become the Girl Scout leader, always prepared, or the very popular president of the PTO, elected for 4 terms in a row. Our phone rang off the hook with questions for that clever Joan O'Callaghan. Throwing on movie-star sunglasses, we hopped into our pink convertible and shouted, "Off to the beach!" Mom was a gardener, a deft seamstress, and a fanatic about laundry, using fabric softener and hanging the sheets outside to dry because they smelled better that way. A whiz with the iron, she put creases in everything. She chose airy white curtains with sunny yellow trim for the kitchen window and pink Swiss dotted ones for my room. She even found some pink chenille throw pillows for my bed. My fantasies had her baking batches of Christmas cookies to give to our teachers and to all of the neighbors. She'd throw great parties and her marinated chicken wings were legendary. She read hundreds of books and took courses at the local college. She loved to play Barbies with me. She sat alongside me while I took a bubble bath, talking with me, smiling, delighted with me. I never had a Barbie but in this fantasy, I had evening gown Barbie, a Ken and a Skipper doll, too. Wrapping me up in a warm towel, my mother combed out my hair, kissed the back of my neck. She helped me with long division. "Don't worry honey," she said, "we'll get through this." She never sent me to school with a fever, with a cold, with a tummy ache. I loved my daydreams, but my lime green dress day was reality, and it would have to do.

When my mother wore her rose dress, she put lilacs in every room. Old coffee cans burst with purple and white blossoms. In her rose dress, she got out of her chair and noticed the small, delicate things. She noticed me.

Delicate and fragile me, able to leap tall buildings, I'd do anything.

When Dad took Mom out to dinner, my brothers and I were enchanted with her. Once a year on their anniversary off they went to The Hollow or Morey Pearls where they had the best-fried clams. Ava Gardner came swishing down the stairs with her Tigress perfume, her pearly blue eye shadow, and her ruby red lips. Out of her housecoat, I saw how beautiful my mother really was.

As soon as I saw the car pull out of the driveway, I made my nosy way into her bureau drawers. I pinned up my hair, sprayed myself with her perfume and spread way too much of her lipstick, Red Rendezvous, on my mouth. Old prayer cards, underwear, and mismatched rhinestone jewelry filled the drawers that smelled of cedar. Mom had the habit of blotting her lipstick on the prayer cards; she never used a tissue. Pillows went unfluffed, beds went unmade, and clothes were everywhere in a heap. There was no time to pay attention because she was always in a hurry. Rushing off to go nowhere, to do nothing. I rummaged through the bureau, frantically, my breathing coming fast. I swallowed hard when I realized once again that there were no surprises, nothing new to be found. There was no special gift tucked way in the back that she was saving to give me, something that I was not supposed to discover. I knew what it would look like, though. A tiny box with a satiny spun ribbon, lovingly tied in a bow with a card: *For my darling daughter, my beautiful baby, on her 16th birthday. Always, Mom.* I wasn't fussy, though. Maybe one of those books about menstruation or a picture from a magazine, an idea for decorating my room. Any just-us-girls thing, something meant just for me. Even a scribble on a scrap of paper to say she wanted to share a secret would have done nicely. She'd be a mom that looked ahead, had a plan for me. I needed to be more prepared. I needed to know all that I could know and should know. What if she went away again and never came back. So I kept digging. Because in her rose dress, I knew she could be that mother and I had great hopes for her. I was just 12 years old; there was plenty of time.

    I took a pair of her panties roughly wiping off the deep crimson lipstick and then guiltily shoved them under a couple of girdles. I was relieved that it was time for bed; worry was exhausting. Stopping first to say a prayer on my knees, I was an over tired baby. Tears brought the sleep that I needed. I hardly heard Dad carry her back into the house but I heard him pack some things and the front door shut again. Easter would come and go and Mom had her ham and raisin gravy in the hospital, miles away from my beautiful outfit and me. My brothers were poking at my hair at Grammy's dinner table, asking if birds lived there. I swore at Colin under my breath so that Auntie wouldn't hear and I told Liam that I'd spit into his food if he didn't shut up. And when the boys started to tattle on me to my grandmother, she just looked at them and said, "Now, now." She looked at me, with a little smile and a glint in her green eyes, and said, "That dress fits you perfectly and isn't it fun to get your hair done every once in a while?" "You look like you could be in the pages of Seventeen magazine. Your mother knows fashion."

    Later that night, I knelt on the soft Oriental rug in my grandmother's room where I would spend the night. "Dear God, I don't know what I did to deserve such a grandmother, but I thank you because someday I'm going to be a lady just like her. Although, I will never get my hair done like this again. Next time, I would like to try a chignon. Good night, God. Take care of Mom."

CHAPTER 3

"Dear St. Luke, the doctor. This probably isn't your field but you must have some connections. Please send some healing, the kind for the soul."

I was my mother's "little psychiatrist," at least that's what my father called me. It worked for him and I liked the title, such authority for a young girl. It made me feel significant in a way that I didn't. I was consulted when my mother had a "sad day." I was on call, ready to drop whatever I was doing; my mother was more important than anything else. School got in the way. In class, reading, playing with my paint by numbers...it didn't matter, one ear was always tuned in to her. Wherever she was, I was on the alert. The FBI needed a girl like me, double-agent Kate, running on rooftops in four-inch heels and glamorous skin-tight black pants, swinging from one high-rise to another, shooting foreign assassins with a steady hand. It would have been child's play for me. Determination was my middle name.

I was Coach Kate, providing inspirational locker-room chats, leading Mom to victory. I paced in front of her sprawled figure, hands behind my back, and told her all of the reasons why she should be happy. *Someday*, I'd cheerlead, *if you try hard enough, you might even be happy without your pills!* I was Tony Robbins, Carol Burnett, Jesse Jackson, and Lucille Ball all rolled into one right there in our 1950's parlor. A comedienne in my plaid jumper and yesterday's underwear, I did impressions of my mother, the way she shuffled around in her robe and slippers. Blind faith pushed me to show her in the only ways I knew. I believed that if she could just see the craziness of it all she'd want to change. My antics occasionally teased a smile from her, but nothing lasting. Depleted, with homework to do, I climbed the stairs vowing to try harder the next time. Psychiatrists didn't always get it right. I knew that even then. Tomorrow was another day, and it was *my* job, not hers, to try and fix it all. She had enough problems.

My mother's rose dress hadn't been seen in a while when a pounding in my ear woke me in the middle of the night, another ear infection untreated. Needing a drink of water, I hung on to the banister and walked downstairs. My mother was lying on the floor, breathing so slowly. She had one slipper on, the other across the room, like a fluffy pink neon sign against the worn brown rug. Two red pills still in her hand, my mother lay motionless. On purpose, she did this, she meant to. But I'd forgive her in an instant if she would just wake up.

My eardrum burst and hot fluid like lava poured down my cheek onto the collar of my nightgown. It must have been the pain ripping through my head so loudly that made my father come running. The banister barely held me up as he rushed by. He knelt beside her, the phone dragged off the table in his hand. He was crying too much to do the job. I lifted his fingers from the receiver and called my aunt. I picked up the stray pink slipper and put it on my mother's foot. Soon the ambulance came and took her away. Two huge men smiled at me and said everything would be all right. They drove down Brantwood Road with flashing lights and no sound. It was 2 a.m. She would have known we wouldn't wake until it was too late. Sitting at the kitchen table, I lay my head down in my hands, too heavy to support. I shook with chills of fever and despair.

All of those wise lectures I had so sincerely delivered, from a child who hadn't lived long enough to know anything at all, had meant nothing. Shivering in my damp nightgown, I whispered a prayer of thanks that I had woken up. It would be years before I slept through the night again. The aching in my head was nothing like the pain in my heart that beat with questions of why my mother didn't love me.

My mother might have been gone forever this time; in a way she was. Her eyes, the color of my favorite cornflower crayon, came back lifeless and gray. Each depression set in deeper and each time she left I was a little less whole. I lost more and more of myself, sending parts of myself with her to keep her safe, to keep her coming back. She lost weight and so did I. She couldn't cry and I couldn't stop.

While she was gone I selfishly wished she were there to see me in my Cinderella costume on Halloween. My blue satin store-bought costume with its garish plastic mask made it hard to breathe, but I loved being out after dark. I was getting older now so this would probably be the last time I dressed up but maybe I could be in charge of bringing Colin and Liam out for trick or treating. I joined the neighborhood kids and came home with a big pile of candy. Dad let us bob for apples until we were soaking wet and had found all the nickels and dimes he'd set inside the crisp skin. Blindfolded, we took bites from the powdered donuts he hung from a string. Sugar flew everywhere as the messy treats swung to and fro. The family camera was always out of film and never worked anyway. The moments would have to be remembered. I took mental snapshots to fill my mother in on what she was missing. She pretended to listen—or at least I thought she did—but she looked as if she were somewhere else. I knew she couldn't hear the running dialogue behind my eyes, the one that said, *One minute I'm too much for you to handle and the next you swallow me up; I can't make you want me. Please want me.*

I buried the worry that maybe needing too much from her was the reason she kept going away. My grandmother told me I had the heart of a Jack Russell terrier; I put my teeth into something, hung on for dear life, and never let go. She thought this was a good thing. But without anyone holding the other end, there was no reason to tug, no reason to fight.

I didn't let it stop me. If I hadn't been so shy I would have growled out loud with the effort.

Mom came home from her hospital stays worse instead of better, little burn marks on her temples from the shock therapy. She shuffled when she walked; the wiggle was gone. I didn't understand what it all meant, but I pictured an electrical outlet and a light going on. It made sense to me that they would try to jolt her back to life, bring light back into her eyes. Instead she slept a lot and smoked too much. When she was too tired to go upstairs to use the bathroom she peed in one of the kitchen cups, the green one with the bamboo trim. I hid a cup for myself behind the shrimp cocktail glasses.

She forgot things, too. I was afraid she'd forget who I was. Television shows were full of dramas about people with "temporary" amnesia. Not funny at all when I worried I'd be forgotten.

My father worked two jobs; insurance company by day, selling men's' suits at night. Every Tuesday he went to night classes at Northeastern University. In the beginning he was always in a good mood, happy to be home after work. In the mornings, I sat on the toilet and watched him shave, joining in his off-key rendition of *'O Sole Mio*. With his finger he dotted my nose with Barbisol, then winked at me and called me his Kitty Kat. On Sundays he went to the Winter Gardens in Cohasset to play hockey while we slept. He loved the game so much that he was willing to crawl out of his warm bed at midnight, swing his hockey stick for hours, and be up for work the next day after only a couple of hours sleep. Light sleeper that I was, I waited until the headlights of his car shone on my ceiling to let me know he was home before I could close my eyes, my shift ended.

Some nights I heard him crying and I wished it were because they'd lost the game. He drank beer when he was sad, and prayed a lot, out loud. He was afraid of something and I assumed it was because of "the phone call." He never told me who it was, but I knew it was about giving us kids up. Listening from the top of the stairs I'd heard him say several times, "When hell freezes over." "She's a good mother, she's just having a rough time right now. The doctors say that maybe this time she'll snap out of it. I know she will. She has to." He hung up and sobbed.

 It took me two months to memorize the *Apostle's Creed*. When he could, Dad sat at the edge of my bed listening, making me start over every time I missed a line. Mom couldn't remember her prayers lately and I needed to know the prayer by heart to receive my first Communion. My father wore a medal that said, "I am a Catholic, please call a priest." He collected the money during the offertory at Mass every Sunday in his blue suit. He was very handsome and usually I was very proud of him except when he picked his nose while driving or during Mass.

 Sister Assunta, my Sunday-school teacher, looked exactly like Ernest Borgnine. The stiff starchy habit cut into her forehead, leaving thick red creases. She smelled like Pine Sol and her neck jiggled like the wild turkeys that ran through our back yard. Layers and layers of black nun dress covered her huge frame, the waist cinched with twelve pairs of rosary beads. I apologized to Jesus for wanting to know what was under that dress. I imagined a pair of bleached scratchy men's boxer shorts with "Sunday" written all over them. In a catechism-induced daze, I pretended that Jesus was sitting three rows in back of me on Sunday mornings. In his glowing white robe, he crossed his legs, leaned back in the chair, and listened to Ernie. His patient soft brown eyes lovingly urged her to go on until he couldn't stand it anymore. He was Jesus and he had given it plenty of time. Then he stroked his perfect beard, cleared his throat politely and stood. When Sister finally noticed him she was struck dumb. The Master said, "This is not how it's done, this is not how I wanted it. Come to me, my children."

We ran and gathered around him and I sat in his lap, my head on his shoulder, inhaling his holiness. I needed a miracle, my own, personal divine rescue.

Jesus whispered to me, "My little one, talk to me whenever you need to, even while you lie awake at night. I will always be there. I will never leave you. I'll help you with those prayers. You need to catch up on your sleep. I'm in charge, *Morning Glory* and I will never leave you. I love you."

CHAPTER 4

"Dear St. Catherine Laboure, are you the one in charge of nurses? Please let this mean school nurse see how really sick I am. I'm sorry; you know I'm not really sick, I don't mean to lie. It's just that I have to be sure that my mother is ok and I can't do that while I'm here at school. Thanks for understanding. Oh, and do I always have to kneel when I pray? This girl's room floor is very sticky. Thank you, St. Kate, you don't mind if I call you that, do you?"

The school nurse and I got to know each other very well—not in a friendly way, but out of habit. I had a different kind of cough, ache, or pain most every day of the week. She rolled her eyes every time I came through her door, and said, "What is it this time, Kate?"

She could have been an army general. Her nurse's cap was like a muffin cup pinned to a bee's nest. Big blue purple veins popped out of the back of her hands and legs. When she walked down the halls, her thighs rubbed together in their white stockings, disturbing my concentration. Her breath smelled like sour milk and her skin curdled up between her buttons, showing her big Sears special-order bra. Her chin looked like my father's when he didn't shave on the weekends. The more I stared at her beard, the more questions ran through my mind. How did her husband kiss her? Not that I knew she was married, of course, but it was possible. Ugly people married ugly people all the time, didn't they? On the other hand, maybe she lived with a bunch of cats. They wouldn't notice that kind of thing. I thought about saying something to her about it, the way you'd tell someone if there was food between her teeth. She had special radar that caught me looking at it time and time again. When she stared at me her eyes burned a hole right through me. Her x-ray vision and my fear of her power were strong deterrents, but I was equally if not more determined than she was. I had a critical objective and would not be dissuaded.

The pain in my ear that I'd had the night before had gotten much worse. My headache felt like I was being stabbed in the head. My foot was cramping up and I couldn't walk. I explained that what I needed was to go home and rest; a little soup should do the trick. Sometimes I had to double over to get my point across and mutter something convincing about appendicitis.

In the beginning, Nurse Birnbaum drove me home, her car the biggest black ride I'd ever seen, like one of those Gestapo cars in the war movies that the Nazis drove, scary and imposing. Silent the whole way to my house, she looked disgusted as I struggled to close the heavy car door behind me. Mom was always waiting at the window. Nurse "Beardsly" had called to say I was sick again, that she was on her way. I put on my pajamas and my mother took a nap. I was on my own, but I was home, sure of what was. One day I was dropped off and the nurse didn't check to see if my mother was there. I had pretended to have 'flu symptoms' that day. My mother had been up the whole night before, my father, too. The house was empty this morning and so I made Jiffy Pop and watched TV all day. A terrible thunderstorm rolled in. I got into my bed under the covers, afraid of the crashing thunder and wind. Luckily I had thought to call my father at work before we lost power. I told him I was home and he told me that Mom would not be home for a while. He said he'd be late coming home but to make sure that the boys did their homework and that Aunt Helen would be by to give us dinner.

Mom could have picked me up at school but she was afraid to drive. My father had tried to teach her years before. The story goes that she was doing all right until she took down an entire white picket fence the length of an entire side street somewhere on Route 53. The people came out of their houses and stopped their cars to see the fence dragging behind our car. My mother was so embarrassed that she jumped from the car and started running down the street. My dad got behind the wheel of the broken-down Dodge Dart of my childhood, picked her up and brought her home, the hanging bumper scraping loudly all the way.

My father said that I should stop going to the school nurse unless I was really sick. "There's nothing you can do, Kate. Your job is to go to school and do well. They're going to keep you back if you miss any more days." Somehow I made it through my school days and then ran from the bus to our back door to make sure that nothing had changed while I'd been gone. Lots of days Mom was there and things were the same. And I was glad that Dad had noticed what I was doing. I felt less alone.

Getting off the bus one rainy and balmy afternoon, I stopped with the other kids to play with the bloodsuckers in the deep puddles. The sun was just breaking through the clouds and a rainbow stretched itself across the April sky. One of the kids shared a bag of chips and we sat on the curb with our jackets off. The forsythias were in bloom and it was unusually warm. Lulled by the normalcy I forgot my job.

When I remembered, I licked my salty fingers, jumped to my feet, and ran home, stopping to grab a crocus from the Delaney's' lawn. When I saw Grammy, my father's mother, at the door my heart sank. I cursed the stupid school nurse and I cursed myself for stopping at the puddle, stopping to pick a stupid crocus and forgetting my job. Grammy held me, her sweet Coty powder making my eyes close. Breathing deeply into her apron, I was like one of the limp rag dolls my mother made for me at the nervous hospital. Grammy's presence meant my mother was gone, but for a while at least my brothers and I would smell supper cooking. Stacks of clean clothes would be put away and there would be fresh tuna sandwiches for lunch.

Grammy always wore an apron to keep her dresses nice. I loved that about her. It was important to her to keep things nice, to take care of things like she took care of me.

My Aunt Helen, Grammy's only daughter, filled in too. She taught school all day and then came over our house to cook and clean. She helped with homework and made me feel smart. And she was very smart so I figured she must have been right when she said, "Someday, Kate, you'll go to a great college. Keep reading the way you do. It will make all the difference." My great aunt, Grammy's sister, was an expert with needle and thread. When she came she made her perfect gravy and buttery parslied carrots. We called her Auntie, too. She was stern but loving and taught me manners, to speak up and to stand up straight.

Grammy, Aunt Helen and my Great Aunt Anna all lived together in a stately Dorchester house in a section called Savin Hill. There was a massive chestnut tree that brought shade to a beautiful screened in porch that I loved. On weekends and school vacations it was my home away from home. Every weekend they went to church where Helen sang in the choir and played piano. There was a statue of the Blessed Mother in their garden. I'd whisper 'good night' to her when I'd sleep over, her beautiful holy body bathed in moonlight. Holy water sat just inside the front door and I put it on liberally, like perfume. They were kind to my mother and if they were angry with her, it didn't show.

We had one especially magical Christmas Eve at Grammy's house. My room was at the top of a long gleaming banister of curving stairs. I called it the presidential suite. Secretary of State, Kate, really loved the accommodations. The room was kept on the chilly side but the sun streamed in the elegant windows. All of the windows in Grammy's house had a seat. The bed was big enough for six of me and the sheets were starchy and clean. Grammy's brother had stayed there when he was sick. I lay in bed at night hoping he hadn't died there, too, but I didn't want to ask. The bathroom outside of my door was a ballroom with hand lotions; pink for girls, blue for boys. There was a long chain with a wooden knob at the end to flush. It made me wonder if our blue toilet at home with it's tiny, cheap stainless handle really did the job. One day our toilet overflowed, the water going down the hallway like a river, around the corner and even down the hardwood stairs. My father had to take the toilet off and he brought it out onto the front lawn to work on it. All of the neighborhood Dads in their Saturday t-shirts came to help. There were three 'D' sized batteries stuck in there, the same ones that were used in my Chatty Kathy doll. My brothers were at it again, no doubt.

Sleep usually came easily at Grammy's, except when we were waiting for Santa. Snow was falling hard this magical Christmas Eve; the night I heard Santa landing on the roof. I flew out of bed, tripping on the bed skirt on my way to go wake my brothers. Auntie caught me in the hallway, hairnet over a thousand curlers, and shushed me back to bed. I got down on my cold knees before crawling back in, thanking Santa for finding us at Grammy's house. In the rush to leave our own house in the middle of the night, our half-decorated Christmas tree had been left alone and I hadn't had time to leave a note. I was worried we'd be forgotten. Santa felt like God at Christmas time and I imagined that they were related.

Mom was let out for a short visit on Christmas Day. She hardly touched her turkey but had a big piece of red velvet cake. She scared me, all skinny and shaky, and I felt guilty that I wanted to indulge myself in Christmas joy. When she had to leave, I hugged her bones and asked when she'd be coming home. Auntie took me by the shoulders and pointed me toward the ribbon candy on the dining room table to save Mom from having to answer. My mother and I said a brief watery goodbye with our eyes.

We stayed the week with Grammy and my aunts. We had cold Mott's apple juice and grapefruit with sugar and toast with melted butter—no Lucky Charms in Grammy's kitchen. Lunch was served promptly at noon, followed by a walk to Malibu Beach or over to Castle Island. Grammy's raincoat pocket, full of sour balls and fresh tissues, still had room for the perfect chestnut. We said prayers to our guardian angels before bed, soothed by the sound of the trains pulling in and out of the nearby station.

I missed my mother but I wanted this too, Christmas away in a warm home smelling of vanilla and roast beef. Being at Grammy's was like being between the pages of a classic book having recently discovered how much I loved to read. I wanted to lose myself in the words, my body held by a green and gold brocade sofa.

CHAPTER 5

"Dear St. Therese. I hear that you're the saint called, 'Little Flower,' and that even as a young girl you loved God so much. I do, too. I'm going to try to be like you today. My grandmother says you are capable of miracles. Dearest Little Flower, let everything be ok. I know that you don't know me but you could ask around. Thank you. I love roses, too."

It was almost 80 degrees. I pulled my hair into a sweaty ponytail and knelt on the soft grass under the willow tree in my neighbor's back yard. They worked every day at the Thompson's Farm Stand and only their tiny calico cat watched me from their window. I thought that willow trees had special powers. I was counting on that, too.

Summer meant being close to home, open windows, wearing shorts and my favorite red Keds. Kids were plentiful on Brantwood Road, where everyone played together no matter what age, one big family. Medium-sized garrison homes bought by fathers on the GI bill, were white with green shutters or green with white shutters. Most had rusty aluminum swing sets in the yard and every family had a dog. We kept cool running through sprinklers in the afternoon and licking blue raspberry popsicles from the ice cream man at night. My toes were stained from newly cut grass. After supper, sweaty games of hide and seek kept us happily busy until dark. I had the best bike in the neighborhood, a Stingray with a glittery turquoise banana seat. Our caravan of bikes excluded no one; tricycles and big bikes alike were welcome to join the parade. We rounded the street several times a day. Baseball cards, fastened to the spokes with clothespins, flapped loudly, announcing the motorcade of Bazooka-chewing pals. We picked blueberries and carried them home in the hammock of the bottom of our t-shirts. One day, my brother Colin turned over a long, mossy log in the woods behind our house during one of our neighborhood exploring treks. Twelve of us were looking for clues to lost civilizations and instead we found 'the land of the yellow jackets' and Colin and Jeffrey from next door landed in the hospital. Jeffrey was worse off because as he ran screaming, he swallowed a swarm of the stinging nasty bees. Every day had a story of its' own. I could be the little girl I was, with a sunburned nose and a mouth that couldn't stop smiling.

When my mother was gone during the summer it didn't hurt so much. Summer was gentler, forgiving me for not knowing when she was in trouble. When it was my turn to count during hide and seek, I got to sneak into the house to check on her or run home for a drink of water, just to see. Still, there were times when she left in the middle of the night while I slept. I slept hard after all that play. I was too tired to hear anything. Summer let me sleep. Jesus said that I needed it.

Holding a cold Coke from the refrigerator to my head, one ninety-degree day I walked to my other grandmother's house. Nana lived just one street over with my mother's three sisters. It was a tiny brick red Cape with white trim, just one bathroom for everyone. From the yard I heard them arguing through the open windows, saying mean things about my father and mother. *She never should have married that 'kraut'. Who does he think he is, uppity mucky muck from Savin Hill? If she had just kept her legs together, she wouldn't have had all those kids. She can't even take care of herself, never mind them.* I pressed my face against the screen door and said hello. A quick "Shush" and hush was all I heard next. I was in my bathing suit so I walked toward the big pool in the backyard. Struggling to reach over the metal sides, I lowered myself in. My suit was two years old, way too small for me. I wasn't allowed to wear a two-piece, though, and rather than fight about it I wore the suit with the fishes in sunglasses on it. The chilly clear water, a relief on this sweltering day, made me shiver. Not much of a swimmer, I held onto the sides, walking the perimeter of the pool hard enough to make a little whirlpool. I loved to watch stories on TV that had people trapped in quicksand. I pretended that I was on safari and was crossing rough waters, the only way to get to the other side by sundown. With my nylon-covered belly leading, I tried to walk against the steady current I was making to see how strong I was; Cairo Kate, Queen of the Snake Infested Nile. Suddenly I lost my balance and was thrown off course, ending up in the middle with the cool water well over my head. I swam upwards, panicking, screaming for help when I broke the water, and then went under again. I was in real trouble and I didn't know how to get out of it. After a couple more times, I began to weaken. I couldn't breathe and chlorine was burning my throat. I said a watery prayer that someone would look out of the window and see me. I thought about drowning in this lonely backyard pool—nothing as exciting as being caught in a riptide or being run over by a bus. No, just a four-foot-deep Sears's pool with leaves on the slimy bottom. I saw my parents crying over my body and worried that my mother would take it too hard. I saw Mrs. Sparrow's second grade class list with my name crossed out in red. I knew I'd miss my brother Colin the most. If Grammy were here, I wouldn't be in this kind of trouble. She'd have pulled up a chair to watch me swim. She'd have said, "Don't get into that pool until I come outside." My throat filled with water and my arms were like jelly. I had no more strength.

I let myself kneel down on the bottom and gave up. It wasn't the first time I'd felt like this but I just wasn't strong enough.

Just then, a force, a tug, gripped my arms pulling me up until I saw the sky overhead. I was swiftly lifted to the surface, choking and sputtering. My heart, hurting deep in my chest, beat fiercely with life. I sat on the edge of the pool, holding on, looking for who had saved me, but there was no one there. I held my hand to my chest and pressed until the calm returned, but I was confused and dazed, unable to find my rescuer. Deep red marks under my arms where I had been lifted would leave bruises.

I heard the arguing from the kitchen windows. The spell broke. Climbing from the pool, my long wet hair in my eyes, I took myself, shivering uncontrollably, into the house and walked past the fighting women. No one said a word. I was nothing more than a cool vapor leaving damp footprints across the angry kitchen floor.

I stood near, the water dripping off my body making a puddle on the floor, and listened to their conversation. At the end of the summer, they said, my family was moving to the city. My mother's doctor, the psychiatrist, said that my mother needed to be closer to public transportation. They snorted and cackled as they imitated him, "This move may help her frame of mind and might help her to become more independent." "It won't help her," one of them said, "Once a nut, always a nut. Good luck to those kids."

I know that my aunts loved me but I felt invisible to them; selfishly forgotten each time my mother went away. It wasn't entirely true, of course. Estelle occasionally painted my nails when she was in the mood. Fran bought me candy, Necco wafers, which I hated. Beth made me thick bologna sandwiches, and said under her breath, "You're as beautiful as your mother. I just hope you don't turn out like her." Fran's husband Joe lived there, too. Joe photographed weddings and called me "his little lobster" when I blushed. Joe made me steak and eggs if I walked over at breakfast time and that's how I knew he loved me.

My grandfather lived in this tiny home, too, and Beth's boy, my cousin Harold. Beth was divorced and Harold was spoiled by all of them. I loved my aunt Beth. She was beautiful with eyes the color of robin's eggs. Papa stayed in the basement mostly, drinking, and Nana sat in a rocker staring out the window, her eyes turned upward. She'd never gotten over losing her son, Buddy, a pilot shot down in World War II. She died with him, that's what they said, but the cancer ate away at her bones while she rocked. Papa had cancer, too, but they cured his with a colostomy bag. My mother once told me that everyone in that house was selfish. Only Fran liked my father and thought he was *so* handsome. The rest of them felt otherwise because he had some German blood in his family and "the Germans killed Buddy." They called him "black Irish," whatever that was, another strike against him. My father was the spitting image of Rock Hudson and my mother always said she'd fallen in love with the cleft in his chin. My dad shook his head and said that Rock was as queer as a three-dollar bill.

It turned out that my mother's sisters were right. We were moving. On the day the truck came, I took one last walk to the house where I was invisible. Uncle Joe winked at me as he got in his car and I blushed. No need to go inside, I climbed into the apple tree in Nana's back yard. It was by far the best climbing tree I'd ever seen, with branches that reached to the heavens and welcoming crooks for sitting and watching the goings-on below. Last summer I'd climbed up with a hammer in my pocket, a piece of thick wood, and five nails hanging from my mouth and had constructed my own special seat. From there I could see the house, the pool, St. Helen's church, the corner store, and Breezy Bends, where we bought tomatoes. Today I sat on my seat and said goodbye to the world I knew and cried tears of despair. I was leaving my friends, everything I knew, and everything I hung onto. I didn't want to go to the city. I was a good daughter. I never complained. I did everything they asked me to do. I helped out whenever I could. I worked hard in school and I was trying to speak up more. It had taken years but I was pretty sure that the kids in my class had finally forgotten about the time I threw up all over Mrs. Morrison's desk. My fever had been so high that day that I really did have to go home with Nurse Birnbaum. Nothing was as bad as the time I was sent to school with diarrhea. As much as I tried not to, I had an accident in math class. I slipped out of the room and into the girl's room, filling my soiled underwear with scratchy brown paper towels. I had Brownies after school that day and I was so worn out from being sick. The skin on my bottom was bleeding, so chafed from another couple of accidents. My mother had just come home from another stay and none of my aunts could watch me. I prayed for the final end of the day when I could go home and sit in a hot tub. After the meeting where we made cards for nursing home patients, I left the building just as I heard someone say, "What is that awful smell?" I had to count on making it home by myself on this cool and already dark November night, as I didn't get picked up like the other girls.

I lied to the leader every week. "Oh! There she is," I'd say, running in the direction of a strange car until she'd looked away, then walked home alone. This particular night, after such a long day, sick and now with fever, the tears rolled down my face as I walked slowly to my home. It hadn't felt like a home. I was so sad and so aware of not being cared for. My mother was napping when I came in, the house in darkness. I hid the paper towels and my underwear and skirt in the bottom of the barrel outside of the back door. I filled the tub with Mr. Bubble and warm water, my body stinging, my soul hurting. I filled my clean underwear with baby powder and put on my favorite flannel nightgown. I climbed into my bed and slept until morning. I'd have to come up with an excuse about homework but I was good at that lately. I wished someone had caught on to that. I tried my best, I really did.

I read to Chatty Kathy when we were supposed to read to a parent. I stayed home from birthday parties unless I could walk there, embarrassed by my homemade gifts. The kids at school wanted to know why I didn't bring cupcakes for my birthday the way everybody else did. I told them I had forgotten all twenty-six of them, delicious cocoa-frosted cakes with pink sprinkles, on the kitchen counter. I signed all of my own permission slips and I never invited a friend over. I hardly asked for a thing.

Up in the tree, I looked down into the pool and just for a moment I could see myself at the bottom. I wiped my tears with my shirt and closed my eyes, still heaving with my little-girl grief.

A summery breeze lifted my hair, cooling the back of my neck. I heard the tinkling of a wind chime and a dog barking next door. Everyday sounds, but clearer, more precise, perfected somehow, were reaching my ears, as though just for me. Then, amidst all the supremely ordinary sensations, came a liquid, loving voice reassuring me that all would be well, not only now, but always. I breathed in an overpowering fragrance of roses and raspberries, so delectable it slowed my breathing. Calm spread through me in a wave and held me in a tranquil embrace.

The voice was one I'd heard before in the quiet, the one that came in answer to the fervor of my trusting, childish prayers. It was the voice of all mothers, the Mother of us all, letting me know that she would always be with me. I knew then that somehow she had gotten me out of that pool.

CHAPTER 6

"Dear St. Christopher, I know that some think you're not the saint of safe travels but I believe that once a saint always a saint. I need you, if you don't mind, to help me get my mother out of the house. Just some simple steps, not a great journey or anything. Thank you, Chris."

I knelt beside my bed this time and I clutched my rosary beads for extra measure. It was going to be a tough day.

We were in the city now, but my mother was afraid to board the bus. Holding her hand, I dragged her up the steps and gave the coins to the driver, leading her to a seat. She sat stiffly, her lips twitching the way they did when she was anxious. I gave her notice a couple of stops ahead, but still had to push her out of the seat when our stop came. One day, thinking I was funny, I said, "Well, it's easier than driving, right?" A cold hard stare met my joke. I wanted to show her the Christmas decorations in Quincy Square and I thought we could have lunch. But she said she was tired so I used money that I found in the couch to take a cab home.

Soon she avoided the bus altogether and stayed home. It was easier. The houses in the city were so close together that you could smell the Hamburger Helper next door and hear the silverware scraping the dishes when people ate. Even so, because my mother couldn't hide from all the neighbors, she made a few friends.

Mrs. Kemp was my new teacher and the tallest, thinnest woman I had ever seen, with hair cut just like a man's. I slipped into the classroom on my first day wearing my coveted white go-go boots, hoping to make a perfect first impression. Spending recess alone leaning against a chain-link fence, I pretended I was bored with city life already. Andrea, also a go-go-boot wearer, the most popular girl in class, made it clear I was to leave my boots at home. She called me names and talked behind my back. One day she called me Squinty Eyes one too many times at the bus stop, so I told her that her breath smelled like Black's Creek at low tide. When my father got wind of it he said, "Is your vocabulary so limited that you must swear to get your point across?" Andrea chased me around the schoolyard the next day. When she caught me she dug her nails into my arm and made it bleed. I told the school nurse I needed a tetanus shot but she told me to go back to class.

    Still painfully shy, terrier that I was, I pretended to be courageous. The schoolyard was packed with kids and parents the day I entered the field day dress-up contest. My parents were at home, unaware that they had anywhere to be. My famous Stingray bike had come to the city with me and I had woven red, white, and blue crepe paper through the spokes. I was dressed as a nun with rosary beads around my waist and rode the bike to school with two small flags on my handlebars. A nice patriotic touch, I thought, as it was Memorial Day weekend. My long black skirts kept jamming the bike chain, once sending me into the Hickeys' forsythia bushes, but I won first prize anyway. It was just a ribbon but I taped it to my bedroom wall and would touch it each morning before I went to school. Things started to change for me in the city after that.

    Janet Schow was two years older than I but she liked me anyway. She had the best mother in the whole world. Our back yards shared the same fence, making it easy to see each other every day. Jan's mother's name was Ethel, such a sensible, motherly name. My mother's name was Joan, after Joan of Arc. I wasn't sure I appreciated the connection. Joan of Arc was burned at the stake; sensible Ethel made lemonade from real lemons. She baked Oatmeal cookies with raisins, too. No Wonder bread at Jan's house, only fresh Vienna bread from Grahn's bakery. Ethel always invited me to lunch, serving up bologna, honey, cheese, peanut butter, letting me have some of everything. She put it all on a lazy susan in the center of the table and we all turned it to select whatever we felt like having. Ethel said that we had to have a piece of fruit. She never raised her voice and smelled of clean laundry and starch in her cotton dresses with the flared skirts. Janet said her mother was "mad about plaid." Ethel, a devout Protestant, always said grace, even at lunch. Janet got tired of having me around. She moved on to another best friend, Debbie Newcomb, who said I was just a baby. This meant I couldn't borrow Janet's maroon jeans, the ones that made me look so cool or get invited to supper or lunch. I couldn't go to her church anymore with her or to the beach. I missed her, but I missed Ethel more than I could say.

My next best friend Lauren was only seven years old when her mother died. I kept waiting for her to cry about it, as though it were on her mind every day the way thoughts of my mother were with me. But, she was used to it by now. Lauren's dad called her "the woman of the house," putting her in charge of her four brothers. Lauren couldn't come out to play until the laundry had been done and supper was on the stove. Together we set the table and mixed up the powdered milk for their meal. A kitchen Madonna sat on the table between the salt and peppershakers with a framed picture of Lauren's mother propped against it. Her mother, Annunciata, had come straight from Italy and hadn't spoken much English. But her home, even in her absence, continued to be filled with her special language. I felt sad for Lauren. At least I had a mother. And I felt very creepy about the calendar of girls in bikinis that her father had in his office. I wondered what Annunciata would say about that.

Laughter and silliness kept Lauren and me side by side. Everything made us laugh. Even when her big brother Vincent said that we were "mental" we giggled ourselves silly until our stomachs hurt. She'd call after him, "I know you are, but what am I?" In our own little world, we collected crab apples in a wheelbarrow from all the neighborhood yards. We went to work washing, slicing, and mashing the apples with the intention of distributing our applesauce and becoming millionaires. We took photos of ourselves in goofy poses in the booth at the mall to put on the label. With our earnings we planned to hire a maid for Lauren's family and get a makeover for my mother. Our company headquarters were located in three huge cardboard boxes we'd found in a dumpster outside of the 7-11. We dragged them down the street and put them behind Lauren's garage, covering them with plastic wrap in case of rain. There wasn't much space, but we weren't deterred. Shoulder to shoulder, we were happy with just about everything.

    Lauren's family had a beach house on Cape Cod, in Harwichport. Each summer we spent a week there wearing bikinis and slathered in baby oil. Our hair in twin sets of pigtails, we walked barefoot on the hot sidewalks down to the penny candy store. Most of the attraction was the guy behind the counter. We didn't have the maturity to feel guilty about laughing, even when we found out that the poor man was "retarded." The man's favorite subject was fried clams. Fried clams were stuck in his brain, and it was the answer to any question asked of him. "How much is the morning paper?" someone would ask and he would say, "Fried clams, yep, fried clams". Choking on jawbreakers on our way back, our laughter hurt our sides. Secretly I said a quiet prayer for the fried-clam guy, my shame burning a hole inside me.

    After a day at the beach, we became Mabel and Mildred on the front porch in our rocking chairs. We rocked ourselves into fits of giddiness telling stories of the good old' days, our aching bones, and our lumbago. One night Mabel and Mildred got adventuresome and bought a six-pack of beer to drink on the beach. Drunk as skunks after one Bud, we chewed our way through a pack of Juicy Fruit before weaving our way back to the cottage where Lauren's Dad sat snoring in his plaid Lazy-boy, bible in hand. After Annunciata died, he'd remarried and become a born-again Christian. Lauren said her mother would have had a holy fit if she'd seen us come home like that. Since her father was sure to have his own holy fit, we didn't stop praying until we got to our room where we collapsed on our beds, nauseous and spent.

    Mr. Scarpini's new wife was the crossing guard at our school. As if a bossy, very large mother wasn't bad enough, Lauren ended up with two younger instant step- sisters, too. We ridiculed Betsey Wetsey and Prissy Priscilla mercilessly, but Prissy had enough problems of her own. Her teeth stuck out like a diving board so far that she couldn't shut her lips over them. It was a howl to watch her sleep. But with two more sisters at home Lauren had more help and that meant more free time to spend with me.

    Once when I came home from a week in Harwichport my parents had done over my room as a surprise. Pink curtains draped to the floor and with the sun coming through my room was aglow in a pink wash. I had a new desk, too, and a soft pretty lamp. Summers in Harwichport helped me to forget things, too, like the time I walked into my parents' bedroom without knocking. They told me it had something to do with "love" but it did nothing to dissuade me from my belief that they'd been hurting each other. I ran into the bathroom sobbing while my father struggled to yank his pants back on. The whole idea was confusing and disturbing to a young adolescent girl who dreamed about having the romantic kiss of a lifetime, but nothing more. When I finally figured it out, I was relieved that my parents were still "doing it," what with my mother gone so much of the time and all. I was oddly reassured that they still loved each other and I needed them to.

    On Family Day we visited Mom in the hospital. It was a long drive and I sat in between my brothers trying to read a book while they snuck punches at each other. I never wanted to go. I was mad at this hospital and everyone in it for not doing a better job with my mother. It was tucked in a pine grove, well off the road, in a rich section of Chestnut Hill. Most people couldn't afford to go there and had to go to a place where zombies went. Sometimes when we got there Mom would be dancing with the other patients. No matter what time of day there was some 1940's type music skipping from a record player by the water cooler. She loved to dance and when things were all right my parents used to go every Saturday night to a place called Moseley's on Route 1. The promise of the big swing band and crystal chandeliers put my mother in the mood and into satin midnight-blue spiked heels. Seeing her dance in the hospital, with the flat foam slippers, I don't know who looked crazier, my mother or the Don Knott look-a-like she was with. But I do know it hurt my dad to watch. He was very quiet on the ride home. From the back seat, hungry and worried, I told my Dad, "*you know, everyone says you're very handsome, even my friends.*"

Mom always came home from her stays with all sorts of ridiculous crafty things she made, like the bright orange yarn doll. The yarn doll was nothing more than a head with ten braids and no body; it wasn't a doll for cuddling and it wasn't cute and I hated it, pretending to like it for her sake. She had pasted blue eyes to the yarn and added a red felt mouth. Glue spilled beyond the edges. I was angry at the doll from the nervous hospital. When I was behind closed doors I undid its braids and pulled the hair tight around the place where its neck would have been. I was grateful I wasn't expected to bring the doll anywhere and was allowed to keep her in my room. I put her on my pillow after I made my bed, neatly braiding the yarn again and straightening her out just so. If the rag doll were comfortable at home on the bed, then maybe my mother would be, too. I tried to keep myself together and it took blood, sweat and tears, not cheap yarn.

Winters and the cold permeated every inch of our house. The icy days chilled me, kept me on guard. I loved to ice skate and spent many a Saturday morning at the MDC rink. Certain social rules at the rink applied. Boys who liked you skated close behind until they could reach ahead and steal the stocking cap from your head, hoping for a chase. I felt like my purple and blue stocking cap never attracted the cool boys, only ugly ones. I'd think, "Oh God, let him have it" and I'd skate around with my flattened hair. One day I just stuffed it into the trash barrel with the remains of my hot chocolate until some boy with pimples all over him found it in the lost and found for me the next week. He chased me until I put the stupid thing back on. After a string of freezing days and nights, my father flooded the end of the driveway and at nightfall, when the boys were finished playing hockey, I had it all to myself. I laced up my skates and glided over the surface in the freezing cold. Under a full moon, I imagined that an international coach scouted me and was Olympic bound. People in the stands were astonished and mesmerized with my beauty and grace. My flowing red hair, windblown and full, circled with me as I jumped and spun. I landed perfectly, balanced and poised, on my razor-sharp blades. Commentators watched the performance and praised me, Gold Medalist, Kate, from the Northeast. "The most talented we've seen in years...exquisite...beautiful." I planned to move to Canada where the streets were made of ice, and send money home to those who knew me when.

Sometimes my father tied on his skates and skated toward me, the moon shining on his face. Drunk, he'd burst into my crystalline dream and rob me of my peace. As I skated past him to go back inside, I felt his hot anger shoot at my back. I knew better than to say anything out loud. Only my silent voice could be heard in the pounding between my temples. Goodnight to the wild light of my moon... Hello helplessness.

After the winter thaw, Lauren and I went back to our old tricks. We were in our non-profit phase and first on the agenda was to clean up the creek down the street. We collected polliwogs, raised them up like proud parents, and gave them a good home. Franny, Tommy, Princess, and Felix scared Lauren's stepmother senseless when they jumped out from under every radiator in the house; the sixteen others we kept under Lauren's bed until they outgrew the family nest. Then, shedding tears of separation, we set them free to rejoin their brothers and sisters in their natural habitat, righteous that we'd done the right thing.

Books were our other passion. We read like crazy, scrambling to get to the bookmobile twice a week. We were sure if we got smart enough, we'd get full scholarships to Harvard, move away, and live lives of fame and fortune. The fake eyeglasses we bought at Woolworths were well worth several weeks of allowance because they made us look like the intellectuals we were meant to be. We used our remaining coins to split an order of fries and a Coke. After the ritualistic loud burping (and pretending it was someone else), we headed to Remick's, our favorite department store. Convinced we looked older and more sophisticated than we were, we grabbed as many gowns as we could in our arms and tried them on one by one for the "upcoming prom." Our breasts being virtually nonexistent, the gowns slid down to our waists and fell to the floor. Hysterical with laughter, we tried on dress after dress until the saleswoman with a black mole on her cheek kicked us out. "Come back when you're serious!" she said. Sometimes we'd pretend that we didn't speak English but one day the mole lady called security. That was our cue to head back to the first floor to sample perfumes and makeup, but the saleswoman there was no dummy either. She was ready for us, as usual, and it wasn't long before we'd be on the street again. She didn't appreciate our London accents. I was Petula Clark and Lauren was Lulu. We did this every single Saturday.

One summer we volunteered at a camp called Happy Acres where we worked with the "developmentally challenged" kids, only back then they were called "retarded," without apology. Frightened by our lack of experience, we clung to each other in our efforts to help. One of the boys, Bruce, followed me around all day and called me "Doctor." I played catch with another boy who had seizures all the time, which left me shaky from fear. When Delia, a girl about my age, said that she liked the pin I was wearing, the one that sparkled with rose-red "diamonds," I gave it to her even though it had been a present from Auntie. When camp ended, Delia threw the pin into the lake and laughed at me. The head counselor put her hands on my shoulders and said, "Sometimes it's hard to say goodbye." I guess I understood, but it hurt anyway and I shouldn't have given away another piece of me.

  Lauren and I did everything together and I slept over almost every Saturday night, even though she had just a twin bed in such a tiny room. I loved her Dial soap smell and her frizzy hair, always in the need of taming, much like my own. I'd watch as she wet her hair and carefully secured ten barrettes in a row down each side, saying a prayer for straight locks in the morning. The results were less than hoped for so we saved up and bought hair-straightening kits, but that didn't work either, the chemical smell filling up the house. Mr. Scarpini yelled, "What in heaven's name are you doing in there? You're going to blow up the place." Our hair clumped together in one thick piece, a strong breeze enough to whip it to one side, where it would stay until manhandled back into place. But, how great, not one curl for a month.

  Lauren went off to junior high the year before I did. She made other friends there and except for coming together one random summer night for a slice of Juicy Fruit, I never saw her again.

CHAPTER 7

"Dear St. Jude, people send my mother cards with a picture of you sometimes. I opened one up and learned that you are the saint of hopeless causes. I ripped it up and flushed it down the toilet. I didn't need to think of things in that way. But, if I offended you, I'm sorry. I'm just a girl and I'm trying to do my best and trying not to feel hopeless. Please forgive me and if things are hopeless, do all you can."

The thing about KC and The Sunshine Band was that whether you liked them or not, their songs stayed with you...a good memory or an annoying refrain that drove you crazy. I would sing along, against my will, but somehow happier for it.

That's what I was thinking as I took the turn into the driveway and saw that my father was home. My mother, very still in a bright yellow sweater, was sitting on the stairs, smoking a cigarette, ashes dropping into her lap. My Dad, on the phone, was saying, "We just got word that Joan's mother died. No, no arrangements yet. Yeah, I'll let you know. ...No, not well at all." He looked at me intensely and nodded toward my mother.

I dropped my schoolbooks and went to my mother as I had so many times before, looking to comfort her. This time I understood why she was sad; this time I was confident I could help. But as I hugged her lifeless, limp body and pulled her up by her arms, trying to make them go around my waist, I knew it was too late. I had seen her like this before. Other times I would have gotten up very close to her face, stuck my fingers in my ears, and darted my tongue in and out, but I didn't do that today. She was looking beyond what was in front of her and lost in the gray world. I let her sit. My brothers ran in from school, never noticing a thing, grabbing snacks and baseball mitts, out the door again in a flash. I took the cigarette out of her fingers and dusted the ashes that were burning a hole in her polyester pants. My heart cried out for her, it screamed for her, it wept for her. I said a Hail Mary and begged for anything.

Two weeks later, full of pink pills, my mother went away again, carried out by men from the city ambulance; nice guys, too. They knew my name by now, and shook their heads sadly at me before they took her out. "Hang in there, Kate. She'll be ok. Do good at school, make your mother proud."

This time my mother was gone for months. Losing her was harder; she'd miss the lilacs again. I didn't shed a tear for Nana. I don't remember the funeral but I'm sure I was there. I'm sure that I wore my Easter dress and my navy and white plaid coat and I'm sure that Grammy was by my side. Nana and my mother were all mixed up with each other, though they didn't know how to be together or how to talk to one another. Nana never looked at my mother the way a mother should. I tried to be close to Nana but I never was. She'd draw me in roughly to her apron and it smelled in need of a wash. I don't think she liked me either. She was stale, like she was almost dead. When she laughed, it was a mean laugh, like she never intended to laugh at all, like it was just a sound that slipped out when she wasn't looking. She showed no love for my mother. I used to imagine that someone at the hospital made a mistake the day my mother was born and had given her to Nana instead of the woman who really wanted her. Maybe my mother's 'real' mother would be feeling a certain worry every now and again. She'd have to sit down and she'd put her hand to her heart, wondering if her daughter was happy in her life. And maybe, after a quick cry, she'd go back to hanging fresh laundry, enjoying a breeze full of lily of the valley. They must have loved each other, at least my mother must have, or why else would she be gone this long, hurting this much.

Life went on. We made family visits to the hospital every weekend. Sometimes we were told to go home, that she didn't want to see us, and we turned around and drove the hour back again. I went to school, did all of my homework, and watched old movies. Mom always loved the ones with Cary Grant. *An Affair to Remember* was how I imagined my parents fell in love and Deborah Kerr was my hero, even more so in her wheelchair. Part of me was unable to fully relax, forgetting that I didn't have to get up and count my mother's pills, making sure she wasn't taking more than she should. At the hospital, there'd be a whole separate room for those pills, lots of nurses standing guard, locks and keys, alarms even. Here, there was just a shoebox wrapped in a pillowcase stowed behind the washing machine. I felt as though I had failed her when I realized that she had found them. She would have died, they said, if she had taken just a few more.

    I kept my little AM/FM radio right behind my bed in a little cubby in the headboard. I liked listening to music in the dark. It helped put me to sleep and made me feel less alone, and when I felt myself drifting off all I had to do was reach back and click it off. After a while, my father's sad visits spoiled the music for me and eventually I stopped listening. He would come in to shut the radio off on his way to bed. There was no lock on my bedroom door. I smelled the beer on his breath and pretended I was asleep. He'd leave after awhile. I know he was sad but I couldn't talk to him about it all. I said a prayer for him instead. I thought about how I'd feel if I lost my mother. I felt empty and hollow when she was gone, but only half filled when she was home. This was one of her longest stays away and the sadness and longing was a physical pain rushing through when I least expected it. My heart broke as I began to see my relationship with her more clearly through my weary eyes. It was hard to get up in the morning with the heaviness of it all. I went to sleep fully clothed so when morning came I got to save every precious second in bed before escaping out the door. I got up, chugged some coffee, and waved goodbye to Dad. In my mother's yellow sweater I headed off to school.

St. Agatha's was a few miles away, a longer walk than to the public school. My father worried about the tough kids, "doing drugs" at the junior high, and said I was better off with the nuns. Little did he know that just a few weeks earlier I had written to the sisters of St. Joseph to ask them to take me in, telling them that I had a special relationship with Mary and that I was called to the sisterhood. The sisters wrote back a holy letter thanking me for writing, but reminded me that *my* work was to do well at school and to always obey my parents. They encouraged me to stay in touch, but I didn't plan on it. I'd write to the Pope next time.

My uniform at St. Agatha's helped me to blend in the way they wanted us to and my yellow sweater had to stay on a hook outside the classroom. I walked to school alone, my knees numb and red in the cold—knee socks only, no tights. The walks in fall I kind of enjoyed and I stopped into the Five and Ten sometimes. The changing leaves warmed my heart and I'd find a perfect one and hold it by the stem, twirling it, company for the journey. I laughed to myself as I walked past the street where I tried to collect for UNICEF one year, chased away by a gaggle of geese, dropping my change all over the sidewalk. I loved the smell of wood fires; the logs in our hearth were plastic. On winter nights it was dark before I made it home. I thought being lonely was for old people, a husband without a wife, or children in orphanages unwanted and disliked by the others. But on these cold walks to and from school, my head down, my cheeks wet with tears, I knew loneliness and I prayed to God to take me.

The daily routine kept me going. My grades were good, except for math. My father said math would always be a weakness for me and helping me with it was frustrating for us both. I took an F in English, lying that I wasn't prepared rather than give a presentation in front of the class. The assignment was to choose an article about a world crisis. When the girl ahead of me spoke about hungry children in Ethiopia, I realized that the article I'd chosen about cats that had been poisoned by antifreeze during the recent cold snap wasn't exactly what the sister had had in mind. I had hastily cut the article out at home the night before, late, after having picked up our mother to come home. She couldn't wait another day, my father had said, so we went to the hospital after my father got home from work. He gave us a box of cookies to split for the ride and by the time we got home, I fell asleep on top of my bed. Sister Mary Glennon, veins bulging, told me to take a failing grade and that as punishment I would spend the rest of the week cleaning the girls' room after school. I had A's on all my essays and tests, but that morning's blunder landed me a C for the term. What would she know about anything, about having a family, about worrying or about the love the Blessed Mother had for me. I wished that Mary could walk into that classroom, like a gang leader for the good and stare Sister down. She'd tell her to make sure that she didn't harm a hair on my head. She'd so coolly walk toward the door, her rosary beads hanging low around her beautiful hips, and turn around and say, "And by the way, black's not your color."

  I hated myself for being so shy, for not sticking up for myself when I should, for the blushing, for my shaking hands, for thinking that I wasn't as good as anyone else. I hated my freckles. At night, after brushing my teeth, I lay in the darkness and twisted my long hair around my finger, pulling it out strand by strand. It didn't hurt all that much and was satisfying in a way that made no sense. The hairs rolled around on the hard floor for a while until they joined together in little clumps, attracting each other like protons and neurons, and ended up under my bed and around the bedposts. Once my neighbor noticed the little piles when he was hurrying to pick up his clothes off the floor and I burned with shame. Not about what we were doing, as if that weren't shameful enough—five years older than I was, he'd told me to keep our secret—"it"—a secret "or else"—but about how he'd found out my own secret.

Now he teased me, laughed at me, pointing to the evidence of my pain and I blushed a blotchy red from head to toe.

    I don't know why I did it. Or kept doing it. Any of it. I just knew that by putting myself in another place, looking down on the life I was living, for some reason it felt good to be disconnected, numb, not so alone.

    The church beside my school, habitually empty and still, drew me to it. I visited on my way home, loving the smell of the holy incense. As I kneeled before the statue of the Blessed Virgin, my Mary, her gold and blue form seemed to reach out for me. I willed her to look at me, to coax life into me. I fixed my eyes on her lips and waited for a smile, but it never came. I lit a candle at her feet and I prayed to stop hurting. Each time I got to my feet I whispered, "I'll be back tomorrow" to let her know I was loyal. Being alone was different in this sacred space. It was my own private sanctuary. The quiet in the church comforted me; the presence of the mother led me home.

    Before long, I was singing in the church choir beside a new best friend, a tall girl with a strong voice and long straight hair. Kathleen Riley and I became inseparable, the only thing keeping us apart were the migraines that had replaced the hair pulling and were now making me ill. My head, full of thoughts and worries, often throbbed, pounding and choking me with nausea. There was no sleep for me; my pillow cradled me without relief. The doctors looked for a brain tumor but found none. They suggested counseling, but we never quite made it to the scheduled appointments. In time, I don't remember quite why, my headaches went away and I was listening to my radio again in my favorite nightgown.

CHAPTER 8

"Mary, my other mother, I'm so tired. I could really use a break. The priest at church on Sunday talked about handing over our worries to God. I'd like to take a few days off, so here are all of my worries. I owe you."

My mother was home much more these days. Her pills were a different color, blue, and bigger. We talked about school and boys. The cakes she baked didn't taste like Ethel's, but I loved them just the same. Even dinner was magically appearing on the table each night. She made trays of creamy custard and good Shake and Bake chicken. Her meat sauce was just as good as the Villa Rosa's up the street, even when we had it every other night.

My friends thought it was cool that my mom hung out with us in her housecoat to watch the soaps. Our favorite was *General Hospital.* I thought that now I knew what normal was.

Singing in the folk group at Mass, I could hear my father's voice across the church. He put my sister on his shoulders and she sang with him at the top of her lungs, occasionally getting the words right. I was embarrassed, but proud too. Everyone loved little Colleen. I was responsible for bathing her each night and together we sang like opera stars. If she cried when I rinsed the shampoo from her hair, I distracted her with promises of special hairdos. "Do you want pigtails, a ponytail, or a bun tomorrow for church?" I asked. Last night Colleen grabbed my cheeks, kissed me and shouted, "Pigtails with bows!" Then we raced to her room to pick out a dress for her to wear, her towel falling around her ankles to expose her pink body. I felt bad that my sister's room was mostly bookcases full of National Geographic magazines. It wasn't girly, just a twin bed pushed against the window and an accordion door instead of a real one. She didn't seem to mind and I was grateful that my parents gave me, the oldest, my own space. Colleen practically lived in my room anyway and when I'd get home from school, I could see her tiny navy ked sneaker moving to a Tony Orlando record that she was playing as she reclined on my bed reading Green Eggs and Ham again. I'd sneak up on her, tickle her, and sing, "Knock three times on the ceiling if you want me..." Mom stayed home from church those days; the crowds made her feel faint, but at least she'd walk to the end of the street to make sure Colleen got crossed. Mom never left the house, not even to sit in the back yard but good times meant that she might say yes to a cup of tea next door with Mrs. Biagini.

Being a part of the youth group at church got me out of the house most nights of the week. On Tuesdays, the group of us sat around a table during our Legion of Mary meeting, hiding our irreverence behind our hands. Father Foley stuttered and smelled perpetually of onions. Spit trickled at the corners of his mouth and he sweat profusely, drops of it landing periodically—plunk, plunk—with deadly accuracy on his rosary beads. I swear we never forgot a Tuesday; it was too entertaining to miss. Tommy McNamara was the one to crack up first, and then there was no stopping us; we fell into hysterics like dominos. "D...d...does anyone...does anyone...does anyone need to leave the room?" Fr. Foley asked us, wiping his brow with a huge, stained handkerchief. But all we did was laugh. And I knew it was ok with Mary.

Weekend retreats took us away overnight where we had snowball fights with the priests. Julie, the boss of us all and resident spy, had a big crush on Fr. Fleming. Julie was lucky because she worked in the rectory after school, where she got to see Fr. Fleming's room and ascertain all the juicy details of rectory life. Julie got a lot of prank phone calls when she worked until she told us to knock it off, that she'd get in trouble. In the meantime, though, she kept us on edge with stories of how Bridget, the housekeeper, drank all day and how

Fr. Foley read *Reader's Digest* in the bathroom. We learned that Fr. Fleming wore boxer shorts with guitars on them and that Fr. Sharkey ate a lot of Chinese food. I couldn't speak to Fr. Sharkey without getting hot and red in the face. Fr. Sharkey was chaplain for the Boston Police Department and looked like William Devane, cool and tough in a handsome sort of way. Thank God he left the parish before I got to make a total fool of myself. I used to imagine that he struggled with the idea of leaving the priesthood for me. My next crush was on Chad Everett, the surgeon on *Medical Center*. I sat in front of the TV for an hour every week to stare at him, while my parents made fun of my dreamy smile. At night, I went to sleep dreaming of his kisses as he wheeled me into surgery and then saved my life. I'd be out of my mind if the President had a speech or the Red Sox had a game at the same time that Medical Center was on. It was unbearable.

Julie and I spent all of her rectory money on makeup in Filenes' Basement on Saturdays. Julie generously bought Estee Lauder powder, some for me and some for herself. Julie had a tendency to wear too much eye makeup in an effort to keep people from noticing how fat she was, but I was quick to agree that it helped her look older and more sophisticated. We concluded our weekly jaunts at McDonald's and then it was off to Bailey's for hot-fudge sundaes before we caught the Red Line to Wollaston.

Julie loved to spend her money on us and I pretended to be polite about it. I accepted her lavish spending with gleeful anticipation. After a couple of months of begging and whining, somehow she talked her father into piercing the ears of six of us girls. He was a gynecologist and somehow that made him an expert. I promised my mother that I'd make salad every night for the next six months and vacuum twice a week if she'd get my father to say yes to putting holes in my ears. The way he saw it, "If you were meant to have holes in your earlobes God would have made you that way." My mother proved victorious, however, and when Julie's father squeezed the gun to my ear, I was so ecstatic I swallowed my gum. He had delivered almost all of the babies in the neighborhood for the last 20 years and we giggled a lot about the intimate details he knew of so many women from Wollaston Hill.

My father had rules about lots of other things, too, like bras and sandals. Sandals ruined your feet and you'd have bunions in your twenties. When my mother insisted that it was time for us to get over to Sears to buy me a bra, my father put it off as long as he could. Finally, mortified at having to go bra shopping with my father but deliciously proud, I got my 28A with the bumblebee in the middle. Dad made me wear a tee shirt over it so no one would know. I said, "Why not just wrap me in masking tape a few hundred times around instead?" I was sent to my room with some stern words over that one. But my mother had won two battles for me; I know because I was keeping score.

Dad was growing less and less interested in me, or so it seemed. My good grades and my English teacher's comments about my talent for writing went unnoticed. The newspaper came between us at night. So did the beer. I wasn't his Kitty Kat anymore. But I had a bra, holes in my ears, and if things went according to schedule, a pair of sandals would be on my feet this summer. But growing up wasn't all it was cracked up to be. My father didn't like me anymore and the shame of that realization sat inside me like a lump, right next to my heart.

Still, my pierced ears and I had a great summer. Kathy's grandmother had a sprawling New England farmhouse at Nantasket Beach behind the old Showboat. Looking over the water from across the Bay, you could see Paragon Park and hear the people on the roller coaster screaming. At night, the park was like New York City, all lit up. Kathy and I weren't allowed to go at night so we sat on the rocks eating Jujubes, watching it all, planning our escape. It didn't keep us from getting all dolled up, either, ever in hopes of attracting attention from the opposite sex. We wore halter-tops and mascara, at least when we didn't get caught. In our fantasies, the cute guy who ran the Wild Mouse ride was in love with one of us. Of course, that would be Kathy because she was smarter than me and she could tan. I slathered on the QT lotion until I looked like someone with liver disease, but all I did was burn. I loved Kathy—that was the only name for the feeling I had. Kathy was the leader. She dragged me onto the roller coaster, where my thighs stuck on the hot plastic seat and after a breathless ride, before I could say no; she yanked me back into line to do it again. My life was full of roller coaster rides and Kathy was always there to help me face them. She had a way of seeing me that made me realize how much I needed to be seen. Kathy gave me courage. I'm not sure what I gave her. I didn't know what she liked about me. I didn't know what I liked about me either. All I knew was that with Kathy I was funny and secure and that I wanted to be with her more than I wanted to go to the public high school where I might go to all of the football games, be a cheerleader or maybe even homecoming queen. So, last summer after another game of Skee Ball at the Park, Kathy told me that she had decided to go to Fontbonne Academy. I decided I needed to go, too. A Catholic all-girls school, what a dream, and you got to wear blue jackets with an emblem. My father reluctantly dropped me off the day of the entrance exam with my three number 2 pencils. He told me to do my best and reminded me that Fontbonne would "cost him an arm and a leg." My grandmother and aunts said novenas and my mother lit a candle and sat by it all day. I guess it paid off, too, because we were both accepted and soon Fontbonne became my own private world—a place just for me.

Come fall, Kathy auditioned for the high school choir. She signed me up, never asking, assuming I would follow her lead. Her beautiful voice was met with deafening applause and then my turn came. As I stood in front of Sister Carmella singing *America the Beautiful* without music, I wanted to kill Kathy, not that I would have thought to say no. Sister looked as though she developed a sharp pain somewhere during my rendition, and I'm pretty sure her hand was up at her ear to save it. I rushed to see if my name made it on the choir list anyway, just in case, but when it wasn't there I was secretly relieved. I'd hoped that I'd had nothing to do with Sister's absence the next week. I knew how painful a punctured eardrum could be.

    School was challenging; I needed to give it my all. I wondered if I was an imposter and if I was really as smart as the rest of the girls at this school. Did someone make a mistake in grading the entrance exam? Did I get the wrong acceptance letter? Good things were happening. For so long I was a patchwork of fragments precariously stuck together and each fragment had to choose which piece belonged where and when. No one gently placed or nudged the pieces into place, except maybe Grammy. But, maybe I was coming together as only a beautiful quilt could; designed with loving detail, becoming whole. And I was smiling more than I had in months.

CHAPTER 9

"Dear angels and saints, I can feel you all around me, running beside me, laughing too. I'm loving my life right now. Keep up the good work."

I spent a lot of time looking in the mirror. I searched my side view, my smile, and posed in a pout for any hint or suggestion of something special. The eyes in the glass, green with oddly scattered gold flecks, looked back in an unforgiving stare. Freckles stained my face like gritty mud, especially across the nose my father called a "ski jump." I scrubbed them with lemon juice and a rough towel, but clearly they were there to stay. I longed to know if I was as ugly in everyone else's eyes as I was in my own. I did know, though, that with my hairbrush in hand and my stereo on, I was the true, white Diana Ross. My concerts, reflected in the mirror of my private peach bedroom where I belted out *Stop in the Name of Love* over and over again, were always perfect. Alone in my room, ugly or not, I held a certain private confidence all my own. A captive audience and sold out every time. I flashed a smile, gyrated, and threw the mike into the air. When I caught it, the amazed crowd went crazy. I cried fake crocodile tears when I sang the song about the girl who was ashamed of her mother. It was one of my favorites. When I took a bow I bent from the waist masterfully, shaking my shag haircut that always needed trimming. What met me in the mirror to the sound of "bravo!" was a beautifully coiffed and full pageboy. All I had to do was bend at the waist and toss my head back. The hair that I kept shoving behind my ears and into a rubber band became another piece of the quilt.

The next day I had a new look. My father had never liked my hair and said I had too much of it, and my mother was always telling me to have it thinned out. As soon as I walked onto the bus, all the girls noticed my makeover and with newfound confidence I got the nerve I needed to run for Student Council. That day I knew I was pretty and I would not be ignored.

It felt good to start liking myself. I felt it in my new improved walk and the way I rolled up my uniform skirt at the waist like the popular girls did. Sometimes I brought makeup to school and missed the first bus home along with the other girls so that we could be on the same bus as the BC High boys. Kathy and I slathered on Raspberry Honey Pot lip-gloss as soon as classes ended and somebody always had perfume. It was the perfume counter at Remick's all over again but this time I knew what I was doing. No individual scents here; we were out to have an effect and our Emeraude cloud paved the way as we casually sashayed to the back of the bus en masse. Kathy was the scorekeeper for how many times the boys looked our way.

Kathy knew about my mother but liked her anyway. She seemed to understand what I didn't want to explain. When my father drank too much beer, he teased me without mercy. Sometimes in front of Kathy he looked at the two of us and asked me, "Why can't you be more like her?" My honor roll friend, the one who could sing and play the piano, not at all quiet like me, stared hard at the bottle in his hand and said without hesitation, "Hey, there's no one like Kate. You should be proud." She left my father speechless and I beamed with gratitude. We'd go to my room and study our Latin.

Sister Malvina wore Coke-bottle glasses and reminded everyone of Aunt Clara from Bewitched with a little Mr. Magoo thrown in. I never would have imagined that Latin class could be so fun. Kathy and I laughed until we lost our breath, and then again in the retelling in the cafeteria after class. Kathy was brilliant at bringing us to the edge of being caught in the act. Latin class was more about the joys of stifled hysteria than about poor old Zeus and Homer. Lucky for us, though Sister was bright enough for teaching, she missed the obvious most of the time. One day she asked us to arrange our desks in a large circle to "enhance communication." While she walked back and forth reading from the *The Classics*, Kathy and I kicked lifesavers to each other. Some of the girls looked down their noses at us for our little game of Latin soccer, but we still got A's, so we chose to take the high road. We marveled that Sister was so clueless—and that we were so sneaky—until she stepped on a cherry lifesaver one afternoon and skated across the shiny linoleum to fall smack on her behind. Shocked, the class went still and silent as a tomb. Sister Malvina slowly lowered her glasses onto her nose and directed her eyes from one face to another, searching out the guilty party. Beads of sweat poured off the end of her squeaky clean nose. My face was flushed and hot. Fanning myself with my papers, I prayed for a miracle. Instantly, Kathy's hand shot up to ask a brilliant question about Homer, so brilliant that Sister seemed to forget that she was on the floor at all. She rose up, unbelievably energized by this clever inquiry, and answered her star pupil with the lifesaver still stuck to her black nun shoes. When the bell rang we adjourned to lunch where I laughed so hard my milk came out my nose. Days like that made life worth living.

Unfortunately, my hair didn't carry the weight I thought it did and I wasn't elected to Student Council. I overheard one of the kids saying I was "a good kid" and another that I was the quietest person she ever knew, but also the nicest, so I floated through the day, my feet a foot off the ground anyway. My grades were good, people liked me, boys were starting to notice me, Kathy was my pal, and my mother was doing okay. It was a perfect time.

CHAPTER 10

"Dear St. Phanourios,

I'm on my knees praying to a saint whose name I can hardly pronounce. One of the Greek girls in school had a medal with your name on it. She told me what I needed to do. I made a cake, not from scratch, and before I put it in the oven I said a prayer for your mother. "May your mother be blessed with eternal peace as you come to my aid". Maria said that I should share the cake with seven people but not tell them why. So I did. I'll just wait and I hope that it doesn't matter how it tastes."

After Colleen was born, they told us it was postpartum depression and that she drank too much. Once Mom had had a seizure at the playground behind our house. I just wanted her to push me on the swing, thrilled with myself for getting her to leave the house. I ran to the O'Hanley's house and my friend, Dave called 911. I could always depend on Dave. But that was years ago, now, and none of that had happened this time around, there was no excuse. My parents had stopped going to all of those neighborhood parties. My father doled out her pills and hid the bottles. Ever the vigilant guardian, it was my job after school to babysit Mom, making sure that she stayed out of trouble. She had to get through the school day alone while my father went to work. I couldn't miss any more of my classes. It was too hard to catch up. One day when I came home Mom was complaining that she was tired; by suppertime, she could not cut her meat without help. Her head, swaying on her neck, hung only inches from her plate. She was taking stronger medication at this point and somehow she must have found the new bottles in my father's suit pocket. He hadn't had time, I guess, to hide them after he picked them up from the drug store. I was the one who usually did that. Lakin Square drug was on my way home and the pharmacist, a kindly old gentleman, called me 'Irish Kate, the Beauty of Donegal'. He always asked how I was doing in school and shook his head in what seemed like sadness saying, "This too shall pass. Say your prayers." If he only knew. I called my father at work, asking if he could hurry. We finished our dinner and took our homework with us. My mother slept on my father's lap while he drove her to the hospital. The next time she came home, after another six weeks away, her pills and my father's beer were under lock and key. It would remain our system for years to come. This was depression. This was my mother's life and mine. Deep inside I held a raging fear that I too, someday, would be her.

My brothers could come home from school, have a couple of Devil Dogs, and go out to play. I needed to stay close to my mother and my sister needed me, too. Colleen met me at the door everyday and leapt into my arms. "You were gone too long!" she said, and I agreed. Practically in my back pocket, she was my own precious yarn doll, alive with love. I had resented giving up my only-girl status in the family when she was born, but now, her tiny trusting face turned up to mine, pigtails bouncing, I was filled with a warmth I had never known. I loved my brothers, too and I was happy for them when they'd come in for supper with sweaty faces and baseball mitts. It all wasn't easy for them either but if I could help make things more normal and happy, then that's what I did.

Liam was the baby who came home alone. The first arms he felt were my aunt's, not my mother's. By the time he was seven, I was taking him to his weekly counseling sessions. I loved him so much; I wanted to save him. He hated the long walk to the train station, tired after being in school all day. We always stopped at the corner so I could buy him a packet of Sugar Babies to eat as he stared out the train window on the long ride there and back. He dawdled infuriatingly at our stop, making me pull him along or threaten to leave him there, an impossible choice. In winter I was angry with my mother because his coat was too small. When we were done it was dark. We ran from the doctor's office to the train, trying to outrun the cold. Most days Liam got a chance to play baseball after school or ride his bike, and I was glad. I knew without a doubt that I'd do anything for him, even the homework that he was too tired to complete when we got home.

My mother left yet again. You'd think I'd be used to it, but this time I was unprepared. She had seemed happier and even though supper only took her seconds to cook, at least she made it. She'd laugh at TV shows and she put her lipstick on most mornings and again when my father was due home. I felt that I had a handle on it all. Occasionally, I'd sneak up to my room and lose myself in a book. Maybe she was watching me, too. She knew my schedule and she knew what she could get away with. Depression became the head of the household and it was stronger than anyone.

My life was broken. I felt it was unfixable, beyond repair, a junkyard of shiny things rusted with pain. I was the family dog left at the roadside, abandoned by all the faith and prayer that I clung to every single day. Devoted love and hope, what a waste of time. I knew now I had never really mattered. It had been a farce all along. The outcome was the same, would always be the same.

My father was distant and drinking, my mother in a locked ward. Liam wet his bed most nights and Colin was getting into fights at school and couldn't read yet. Colleen was passed from one babysitter to another while we were at school. I learned that every girl except me was shaving her legs. I learned that kids my age showered every day—not once a week like I thought. I got my first period on the bus on the way home from school. Panicked, I knew I would have to walk past the BC High boy, the boy of my dreams, with a huge wet bloody stain on my skirt. Downey—at least that was the name on his football jacket—was absolutely perfect. He'd never even once looked in my direction, but I saw myself in his jacket with his arm around my shoulders. My stop came first. I thought I'd wait and get off at another stop, after beautiful Downey got off at his. I slouched down in my seat, making myself invisible. But the bus driver was helpful to a fault. He stopped the bus, locked on my eyes in the rearview mirror and said loudly, "This is you, little lady." I slumped as far into my seat as I could get before falling onto the floor. Maybe if I ignored him... But he said it again, louder this time, a question in his eyes. The whole bus was looking at me now. There was nothing I could do to hide it. I held my book bag behind my back and tripped down the bus stairs. My face was on fire with the shame of it. There'd never be a chance for me now, not with this boy.

    I began to hate my mother.

CHAPTER 11

"In nomine Patris et Filii, et Spiritus Sancti. Amen. Maybe a Latin version will get me a little more attention."

    Jeff's leather jacket and cologne made him worldly in a way I knew nothing about. I was sure they were signs that he knew a lot more about everything than I did. We were fifteen, both ready for the *something* all fifteen-year-olds are ready for. On our first date we walked for miles to get to the beach. Jeff took his jacket off for me to sit on and we leaned against the sea wall. It was a freezing cold afternoon, but I was hot with what felt like fever. With the frigid wind whipping around my first kiss I was propelled into Jeff's arms. Sheltered there, worrying if I was doing it right, Jeff called me an angel. We kissed for hours, frozen—literally—in time. Touching his face, my fingertips grazed his whiskers and suddenly I got scared. Whiskers definitely meant that he knew more than I did. But then Jeff put his lips to my hands and covered them with his sweater. I relaxed. He wanted nothing more than this. And I needed to have a life outside of my home. My neighbor had moved away and finally I forgave myself for his transgressions.

    My father said boyfriends were forbidden until I was sixteen, but Jeff tried hard to get on his good side. Sometimes my father pretended that Jeff wasn't even in the room when I invited him over. Jeff paced in front of my father's chair, his cologne wafting behind him in waves, until he could no longer be ignored. Then he was ready with a list of little-known Carl Yastrzemski facts or anything at all about the Bruins. His sports initiative earned him the prize of watching a whole baseball gave with Dad. I wanted to scream. Before I knew it, it was time for Jeff to go home and I hadn't gotten a minute alone with him. As soon as my special boy in his leather jacket left, my father began his campaign. Jeff was "pathetic, pathetically short, overdid it with the aftershave. Who did he think he was,

Frank Sinatra?" I was sad. I loved the smell of Jeff's cologne on my hands and I loved his gentle heart. After I left him I didn't wash my hands unless I had to, and slept with my fingers close to my face. We had nothing to be guilty about, but my father sulked around when we were on the phone, insisting we were "up to something." Sometimes when Jeff and I kissed feelings that were new and wonderful to me warmed me from the inside out. Tingling and stirring feelings that I called love made my eyes shine with something other than tears.

My mother indulged me, called it puppy love. She didn't quite make fun of it or imply it shouldn't be taken seriously. My father stopped talking to me. Neither made much difference.

Years later, long after our puppy love had faded, I remembered how Jeff and I had cared for one another when he and his wife came to visit his father in the hospital where I worked. I was the attending nurse and Jeff's dad was very ill. I had settled Mr. Gosnel in for the night when I opened the curtain around his bed to see Jeff standing there. The man, Jeff, was still shorter than I was. The kind of grease that you can never fully clean from hard-working fingers stained his hands. He told me he was a mechanic now, with his own shop. My father had told me over and over that's all he'd ever amount to. But Jeff proudly told me about his business and his wife held his arm and looked up at him with love. He looked at me with the same kind eyes, bluer than I remembered and tired and moist with sadness, eyes that had once told me how special I was. He touched my nursing pin and said, "Good job, Kate."

His touch instantly recalled the morning we stood in the pouring rain at the bus stop, crying, two fifteen-year-olds, on the day before my sixteenth birthday. I told Jeff that I couldn't see him anymore. My father's silent treatment was killing me. Dirty was not how I wanted to feel, but I did, no matter what the truth was. None of it made sense, but I knew my father didn't love me anymore and I wanted him back. My father and I had lived a partnership that I couldn't be without.

The next time my father disapproved out loud was when I was eighteen. Timmy was a tall, blonde, green-eyed football star who I met at a party that I wasn't supposed to be at. I had told my father I had to work the night shift at the nursing home but instead stayed out all night long with Timmy. I was over the moon that he wanted to date *me*. We were together all summer and I was crazy for him. After he went off to college in Connecticut I spent months sewing him a quilt, king-sized for his twin bed, all by hand. I waited for his calls; they were few and never on time. In October I told my parents I'd be at a friend's house overnight when I had really rented a car to drive down and see Timmy at school. Even though driving on the expressway scared me half to death, and I didn't like doing it alone, I was soon making the two and a half-hour trip whenever I could. I'd found a car rental place in the Combat Zone in downtown Boston that rented to eighteen-year-olds if you put down a hundred fifty-dollar deposit. Each time the car alone took two full paychecks. When I returned it late on Sunday nights, I had to walk to the T and then walk the long two miles home. Timmy never asked about my arrangements. When I was there, I was there; when I wasn't, I wasn't. He called me "doll" and told me I was beautiful. That's all I cared about. Timmy wasn't much of a kisser, I could tell he didn't know how, but again I didn't care. My life for two years was spent on Route 95 in one ratty car after another to see the boy I thought was everything I'd ever wanted. We'd just had our two-year anniversary when Timmy broke up with me. I was crushed, but not for long. Simple heartbreak was easy for me.

I rode the T to Boston to my summer temp job and watched, fascinated, as the people got on and off the train or the streetcar and walked by on their way to do whatever it was they did. I wrapped myself in a cloak of freedom that I earned with the paycheck I got every week. Kathy had gone to college and I was on my own. I'd start at the state college in January. My social calendar was filled with men old enough to be my father. Eighteen and I was going through the motions, all dressed up like a real workingwoman. Wearing lipstick and high heels, I was trying to be someone else. I pretended to have all kinds of experience and told stories about where I went and what I did, made things up right and left. No one caught on, not even at home. I kept them all at a distance, especially my mother.

Everything she did aggravated me. When she walked by me I made sure to sneer at her dirty old slippers. She sat at the kitchen table most of the day hacking and coughing, her face hardly discernible through the constant cloudy haze of cigarette smoke. She had the nerve to ask me to vacuum when I got home from work. When she occasionally bothered to do the laundry, it was as if it hadn't been done at all; the stains were there to stay. She might have done the folding with her hands tied behind her back. She didn't know where the iron was—and had never asked. It sat at the foot of my bed where I used it every morning, cursing her as the steam curled my hair around my face. Wiggly-skinned, boiled chicken and hard, boiled potatoes approximated supper. Sometimes potato pancakes with ice-cold centers for a "treat." My brothers' idea of fun was to stuff their mouths with potato and then slap their cheeks—potato everywhere, on the walls, table, and floor. I was not above getting into the act either, drinking milk as though I'd had a stroke, letting it spill in a gush down my chin. Vegetables appeared only on Sunday when Dad cooked. I didn't really miss them. I missed the sound of my mother's voice telling me what was good for me. I missed hearing how carrots would help my eyes and how spinach would make me strong. Because I didn't know, but I guess she didn't either. I needed her to care for me. And I really needed her to know how I was living my life.

There was a time that being sick worked. When I was sick my mother acted more like a mother, almost as if my not feeling well lifted her burden and gave her a brief respite into the foreign and mysterious world of happiness. I could tell that she needed to feel like a mother. I wanted to appreciate the good, I really did. With her cool clammy hand on my forehead, she rose to the occasion and I got the day off. She fell for my sick act every time, even well into my high school years. I lay on the couch with my pillow and blanket, blissfully content. It was just toast, ginger ale, and Lucille Ball stuffing chocolates into her mouth and down her dress. I knew enough to choose rainy days when the house was naturally darker and only a light or two got turned on. My mother was at my beck and call and other than catering to my wants she stayed in the living room with me all day. When Helen, the neighbor from next door, called my mother said, "I can't talk, Helen, I have Kate home sick." I tried to hide my pleasure and look sicker. My mother rolled her eyes at the sound of Helen's voice; Helen always had too much to say. And in those moments we were bound by an indiscreet knowledge, a secret, and I swooned with the complicity. These were times when my mother couldn't pass up the chance to be the mother she wanted to be, and I let her. I needed her to be that mother.

The downside to all the faking eventually surfaced when I was sixteen. My rather unique collection of symptoms was drawing a lot of attention and soon I was being examined, prodded, tested, and analyzed, all to no avail. My mother, rife with indecision, didn't know what to do. One day I found myself in a cab on the way to have another test, a Barium enema or a CT scan or something else the doctor suggested. Ultimately I was diagnosed with high blood pressure, as if it didn't matter what the diagnosis was as long as they found one. That's when I decided it was probably time to quit. Letting her make it all up to me was giving me more of a headache than it was worth.

The last time she sent me to the doctor, my senior year in high school, he asked me what I wanted to study in college. I told him that I had a real sense about people and my plan was to be a psychiatrist. His wrinkled paunchy face scowled down at me, "That's just a symptom," he said, without explanation. Then he wrote me a prescription for Librium. Take one as needed, it said. I stuffed it in my pocket. Dr. Torell was the same doctor who treated my father in the next few years, completely missing a heart attack waiting to happen.

CHAPTER 12

"Dear St. Mary Magdalene. I know you didn't have the greatest reputation but take it from me, I know you tried. You just wanted to be loved. Maybe I could ask you for a blessing. We could be like sisters, you and I. You'd be the oldest and I'd be the one learning from your mistakes."

I hated it at the State College. I had no friends and was eating my lunch alone. I spent all my time in the study hall writing letters to Kathy. I skipped classes. I finished out the year with an A in Anthropology and flunked everything else, including psychology. I gave up my grandiose dream to be a doctor and applied to nursing school. My happier days in high school seemed a lifetime away. I was lost again and I didn't want to go back to high-heeled shoes.

A friend was going off to nursing school and I decided that maybe that's where I belonged, too. An acceptable career pursuit for a girl, I guess, because no one said it was a "symptom" this time. The reaction to my newly formed plans pleased me. Grammy was proud, Helen and Auntie, too. I took a job at a nursing home, close to my house, so that I could walk there. Elmwood Nursing Home was known as "nursing boot-camp" for aides. I spent the summer before nursing school in their kitchen as the suppertime cook, but I was fired for putting cheese in the tomato soup to dress it up a little. The menu was *not* to be altered." I begged the administrator to keep me on, said I'd do just about anything. Finally he gave in and hired me as a nursing assistant. The head nurse balked at his decision; she's the one who'd wanted me fired. But I didn't care. Mrs. Baldwin was a bad nurse with rancid boy odor. The April Showers perfume she doused herself with did nothing more than draw attention to the odors she was trying to hide. I used it to my advantage, working it skillfully into the conversation when she gave me a hard time. I let her know that lipstick was for the lips, not those yellow teeth of hers, and was rewarded with a glare of intense dislike and internal combustion.

It wasn't long before I got my chance at Nurse Baldwin. I always made it a point to get everything done before she found the time to ask me. One night I had fed Mrs. Judd and cleaned her draining leg ulcers well before the end of my shift at seven, and had performed six more evening backrubs and six more baths, all while the other aides were out smoking pot on the fire escape. I saw my father's car out the window, where he was waiting for me to come out. I was saving for my own car but I had a long way to go. The next thing I knew Nurse Baldwin had called the police, insisting a pervert was lurking outside the Home. When the police arrived and I introduced my father, there was more than enough embarrassment to go around. But this time it was all hers. As I let myself out, I called her a cow under my breath—loudly, hoping she would hear.

There was a well of familiarity at the Elmwood with its odors of old and spent lives. I was comfortable with the tucking-ins, the food cutting, and the wrapping of warm sweaters over frail shoulders. Annabelle believed she was the Elmwood's director. A tall ninety-four-year-old with long white hair down to her hips, a strong British accent, and a bit of a confused outlook, she reminded me of the Ghost of Christmas Past. "Do you need anything, luv?" was her most-used expression, good-naturedly directed toward everyone she met as she shuffled through the halls. Most of the patients responded to her gentleness and her size, willing and ready to believe she was in charge. But Annabelle's good days were fewer than her bad. Minna, on the other hand, was blind and feeble and her head was permanently cocked to one side. She sat in "her corner" all day. From that spot she called invectives to all who passed by. When Annabelle's shuffling reached her ear, she screamed, "Get her away from me! Get her away from me," and Annabelle offered only, oh, so softly, "Oh, so sorry to disturb you, luv." Annabelle took no offense, ever calm and blissfully unaware of the true nature of her surroundings. I knew she had spent her life as a midwife in London and often found myself staring at her huge, capable hands. One Tuesday my chores included laundering the massive amounts of accumulated linens that never let up. Annabelle insisted on helping me, folding each item just so. Impressed, I was caught unaware when she suddenly sat back on the basket of clean towels and promptly urinated, then asked ever so sweetly if I had a "bit of a tissue." Her confusion hurt me, disappointed me. I didn't want it to be so and took it personally. Wearing a dazed and angelic expression, she accepted the crumpled tissue from my pocket as I scolded her. "Annabelle, you just peed all over the towels we just folded!" Annabelle looked at me, shocked, and said with the utter conviction of the deranged, "Oh, no, luv, I'm sure I just couldn't have."

As she left the laundry room, Annabelle turned and asked if I would check in on the Wilson baby and teach his mother how to breastfeed. She had another delivery to attend to, and "this baby wouldn't wait!" Annabelle died in her sleep the week before I left the Elmwood, her hands folded around a prayer card of the Madonna, and when I left for nursing school I took her spirit with me. Another mother had led me back to myself and I gained strength from that embrace.

Tossing and turning until I fell asleep exhausted each night, I thought about the horrible mistakes I might make, the potential for disaster, the lives I might take if I screwed up. I was lucky if I got a few good hours of rest before I woke up, startled, to look at the neon hands of the clock; three in the morning, again. I was waking up on my clinical days like this, my hair curled around my finger, my body slick with sweat and then racked with chills. Pulling the covers over my head I prayed for a little rest but all I heard was the voice of the nursing professor pronouncing, "You're just not nursing material, Ms. O'Callaghan." St. Catherine Laboure School of Nursing was the best nursing school in Boston except for the

City Hospital. Carney Hospital was an average sized community Catholic hospital where sisters in habits roamed the wards offering Communion or ready to hold a hand in prayer. There were crucifixes over each bed and it all brought me a certain comfort. We served the people of South Boston, Dorchester and Roxbury. Back then, we couldn't put a black patient in with a white patient and we spent a lot of time making peace in the hallways.

I stood by my locker in the deserted early morning hallway getting ready for my first day. It smelled like that green powdery stuff the janitor pushed around to clean the floors in elementary school. That strange, sweet, play-doughy-like smell that was supposed to cover up the scent after someone got sick. Thinking I was unobserved, I swallowed the first Librium of the day without water, after weeks of indecision about whether I should fill the prescription. I was just applying the last bobby pin to my hair to keep it under my cap—wisps of it kept escaping because my fingers were shaking so hard—when I heard Nurse Bilbo's voice ricocheting off the walls, "Save those for Saturday night, why don't you." Nurse Bilbo had eyes in the back of her head—under the hundreds of her own bobby pins, that is. I froze, praying that she hadn't seen me actually take my dose of bottled courage. But even that might have been better than the onslaught of angry, red hives I felt cropping up all around my neck. I wanted to sink into the floor. I yanked the collar of my uniform up as far as it would go. "Yes, ma'am," I said demurely as she strode by, her shoes making loud echoing squeaks on the linoleum. *Please, Mary, help me to be a good nurse*, I prayed. *Please, Mary, help me to be a good nurse.* The Librium made me a little foggy; the prayers brought the palest sense of calm. And at least I looked better than Meredith Kaminsky whose neck was covered in hickies, lamely dabbed with Colgate. I was so disappointed in her when I saw that. She looked like she had been attacked by one of those vacuum cleaners at the carwash. I didn't even think she liked that nerdy boy she was going out with.

I rushed into the stairwell and climbed the five flights to 5-North rather than take the same elevator with Nurse Bilbo. Mary Walsh, my head nurse, rushed over when she saw me. "Your first day as a student nurse, how exciting!" Taking a deep breath, I searched her face, grateful for the vote of confidence. Tears were so close. I had met Mary at a wedding and told her that I had applied to Catherine Laboure and that I hoped to work as an aide so that I could have a head start before clinical began. She called me the next week and offered me a job. She had been my guide that summer, my wizard behind the curtain, holding my hand as I dressed Mr. Brown's tracheotomy or put a Foley catheter into Mrs. Lawson. She and the other mother-hen nurses pulled me in and out of rooms to "see this!" or "try that!" They believed in me and it was their belief that carried me through the next few months and another hot summer of work, until I woke up one day to find I'd slept a whole night through. My prayers had been answered. Now on my clinical days I carried their safety net inside me. The Librium went into the trash.

I was the youngest student nurse on the ward and I worked hard. But the words of my father were like buzzing flies around my head. *You'll never make it through nursing school; you'll never make it through nursing school.* I fantasized how he'd "accidentally" come to the floor and spot me. He wouldn't want me to know he was there, of course, so he'd hide behind a cabinet to watch in awe at the spectacular nurse I'd become. Then he'd come out of hiding and congratulate me. He'd eat his words. His mind would be forever changed about me when he witnessed the capable girl who was his daughter. His stomach would turn when he saw the things I had to see and do. He would be dizzy watching me make so many decisions, running from one end of the corridor to the other, answering questions and phone calls, directing patients, holding hands. He'd see me skip lunch in favor of helping with a procedure or because there just wasn't time to eat. From where he stood, he'd instantly see the respect I earned from my peers and from the doctors who thrust sheets of orders at me, thanking me in advance for getting it all done. He'd see all that and more. He'd finally be proud of me and love me again. I wanted to be here. I wore my miraculous medal every day. St. Catherine Laboure, a young nurse, had been visited by the Blessed Mother and asked to fashion a medal of Mary with the words: "O Mary, conceived without sin, pray for us, who have recourse to thee." I felt blessed to be here and I would make Mary proud, too.

Here on the ward I was held to my own impossibly high standards, a consummate over-achiever. But I did it all and did it well. I left each shift with aching legs, but I knew I could hold my head up high.

CHAPTER 13

"Dear St. Catherine Laboure. I love you. Stay with me."

The summer before I graduated nursing school, my father died. I remembered one night when I argued with him about wanting to live on my own someday. I thought it would be great to live with a few other girls, all of us working to pay the rent. He told me that I was selfish and unappreciative and that in our house, girls didn't move out until they got married. I stood tall and said, "Well, not this girl!" He was so mad at me that he chased me up the stairs, past the statue of the Sacred Heart of Jesus. I slammed the door to my bedroom and locked it to his screams of, "You're going to give me a heart attack. You're just like your mother."

He did die of a heart attack at only forty-six years of age. Until I moved out of the family home to get married, I'd walk past that statue and see the blood in Jesus' heart and feel deep regret about that night. I wrote Dad out a card telling him how much I loved him while he was in the hospital. I kissed him and thanked him for everything he had ever given me. I know that he read it in his bed hooked up to so many machines and IV's, before he went into delirium tremors. The last thing he said to me was that he would be joining the gym at the Y when he got out. He also begged me to keep the nurses from cutting off his wedding band. I was only 19.

The whole family had gathered in the Gray waiting area at the Massachusetts General Hospital waiting for word on his surgery. One of the top cardiologists in the country came out and asked which one of us was 'the nurse'. I stood shakily, whispering low that I 'was just a student' and then he told us that my father didn't make it. He turned to me and gave me all of the clinical details, some of which I understood, but most I heard as though I were under water. He said that he was very,

very sorry and he found it hard to face my mother. A huge part of her died, too, right there in front of him. I remember the confusion of what to do next. It didn't seem right to just leave my father here. My mind drifted to the operating room where my father had been. I imagined that he wasn't dead after all, that he was left alone, unhooked himself from everything, put on his black socks and his khaki pants and walked out of the room. I saw him hail a cab and off he went to a new life. I felt that maybe God had given him a break, let him have another crack at life, one in which he wouldn't have to worry about my mother, money, or me. I almost got up to go check, all of it so seemingly more real than the truth that he was gone forever.

It was weeks before I started to cry for my father. My last year in nursing school found me in and out of depression. One day after clinical, I took the bus to our family church, St. Ann's in Wollaston and in the pouring cold fall rain, thinking of the warmth I might find there, I tried to find an open door. The doors were locked, all five of them. Kicking, pulling and banging on the huge mahogany doors, I would not be kept out. Racing from the front door to the side doors to find no entry, there was nothing I could do but lower myself onto the marble steps sobbing and shivering. I prayed for forgiveness, for peace, and for the end of the sadness. I had so much left to do. Hours later, my waterlogged nursing shoes walked me the three miles home and I fell into bed, soggy uniform and all. I slept until morning and the sun set me straight—I had lost my father, my Santa Claus and my partner in the care and watching of my mother. Gone without a trace, no instruction manual left behind; I'd have to figure it out all by myself. Making my way to the closet, hoping that there'd be a fresh uniform hanging there, my arm brushed against the soft sleeve of the last present that my father ever gave to me. I had wanted that rabbit fur jacket with the leather trim for so long. I'd overheard him tell my mother that all I needed now ere some high, spiky boots and a wiggle. I never asked for much and though he didn't want to buy it for me, he did want to give in. I wish I could have told him about the look on the bank teller's face when I went to collect the food stamps in my jacket all those weeks after his death.

As I ironed my uniform for the pinning ceremony the following summer, I thought about how my life had taken me to this exact night. I saw myself walking onto the stage to accept an award for "all my efforts." In a gold sequined cape and sparkling tiara, I'd hold up the trophy and say, Thanks, but no thanks, to all you little people who told me I couldn't do it. The audience, mouths open in silence and aghast, would whisper. How could she say such a thing? They'd demand to know. Then I'd rip off the cape, throw it to some lucky person in the crowd and, holding my hard-earned trophy, stride with great purpose up the middle aisle and out the door, letting it slam satisfyingly behind me.

I was nothing, though, if not polite. I would collect my pin with a nod and a smile. I knew I was a natural. Taking care of others was in my blood, seared into my very skin, and the one thing I knew was that I could trust what I *really* knew. I'd been on call my whole life; the only difference was that now I was answering that call with everything I had—and doing it for a living. On this warm tropical May evening, I carried a rose, blood red, against my very white uniform. For a second, in the mirror, I imagined it was my heart.

I saw that my mother had come to the ceremony, she who had missed my high school graduation entirely. Afterward, she stood with my grandmother and aunts in the crowd outside. I came out of the church and saw her, cigarette in her hand. The warm breeze lifted my hair. Most girls were wearing their hair up, but I had taken special care to style mine so it fell across my shoulders. My golden pin had been secured by Ms. Cremins, my favorite professor, and gleamed in the glow of the dusk. I searched the crowd and for a minute I imagined that I saw my father there, and then he was gone. I saw my newest boyfriend Shane holding flowers, waiting for me. I wanted to stay right where I was, above the crowd, looking down at them, drinking it all in. I wanted to scream out, *this is mine. I did this. I made it.* I had the secret knowing of Mary by my side. I took my time, feeling the goodness of the moment, and then I ran into the crowd.

Now a real nurse, I got paid for all the caring. My schedule was crazy, but I still found time to get engaged to Shane, a plumber at the hospital. His brother had wanted to ask me out, too, but Shane was the braver and had gotten to me first. We sat together on the fire escape on our breaks and kissed in the dark. Shane had insisted on asking my father for my hand in marriage. Shane had been beside me the day my father died. In a rare moment of decorum, the father I loved and feared, pulled out a bottle of scotch and said yes. The men toasted the happy couple and it was done.

Although Dad didn't make it to the wedding, somehow he had managed to save two hundred fifty dollars for me, however, and I bought my wedding gown with the money. It was tucked away in the same place where he had put his life insurance papers that terrible night when he had such chest pain. I needed Shane and I needed to be out of the house where I'd grown up. I'd never live in Harvard Square with the girls, trying my hand at independence. Marriage gave me the excuse to move on, to let my mother find her own way. Everyone said that I was good for Shane, too, that "maybe, finally, he'd calm down." I would be a good influence on him. He had been in trouble a few times with the police, but since he met me he did seem changed. His past was an issue between us but I was intrigued by it, too, the way I'd been with Jeff's cologne and whiskers. Shane knew things. He cajoled me into my first black leather jacket and onto the back of his motorcycle for my first ride. Shane called me Babe and taught me about sex. He had a beard and the longest eyelashes I had ever seen.

I wanted to marry Shane more than anything. I really did. Yet, my heart said, no, don't do this. I had discovered that Shane and I had different definitions for lying. His contention was that lies of omission weren't really lies at all, simply fibs of convenience. That left him free to be in places where he shouldn't be or said he wouldn't be and to be with people who were trouble. Hurt led to anger until I finally hurled my diamond ring past his head, flooded with relief that I hadn't said, "I do." In one of my psych classes I learned how people in "caring professions" often came from families where they were children forced to be adults. They put others first, always. I knew that's what had happened to me. I kept my distance from him for as long as I could. I needed some caring of my own and I knew that I needed to find it within myself but the guilt took over. I had to please others. I couldn't let anyone down. I had made a promise and I would keep it. I missed Shane. I missed his arm around my shoulders. I needed his love even if I knew that I'd be disappointed from time to time. I also was filled with desire and I knew that if anyone could change Shane, it would be me.

Three months later I succumbed, deadened and dizzy with neediness. I gave in to Shane's pleas and his parents' pressure. *Forgive and forget, Kate*, they said, over and over, *that's what you need to do. He loves you.* I knew they were right, and I'd always been good at that part, the forgiving, and the forgetting. I could still remember the love in Shane's eyes when we first met and the laughter we shared in between the hard times. I loved Shane's steady and sensible parents. They'd be my parents, now. So, two months later, on the hottest day of the summer, I said, "I do" for real. At least I hadn't disappointed anyone.

I focused on my work. My first year of nursing, surrounded by real life pain and suffering, tested my endurance. I tended to eight or ten patients at a time, pulled myself from one to move on to the next, to a new set of problems, a new set of challenges. Always attentive. Always *there*. I was mistreated; I was revered. Making people healthy again wasn't easy. Sometimes I had to hurt them, make them suffer "for their own good," appalled at some of the things I had to do and say. Apologizing, chastising, offering hope... sometimes all at the same time. Applying a painful burn dressing one minute, suctioning the life-stealing fluids from lungs the next. Pumping ice water into the stomachs of bleeding alcoholics, restraining them in their delirium. Sitting at their bedside when they were sobered up, talking to them the way I talked to my mother, I was the cheerleading child again. "Come on, I know you can do it, you just have to try harder." I leapt onto beds to perform CPR, I shouted out orders. I brought our unsuccessful attempts down to the morgue. I spent hours reorienting the demented ones, earning an occasional moment of bright recognition in return. The job demanded of me. I was rejuvenated...elated...utterly spent.

Shane began waking up to an empty bed. I was sleepwalking, hanging up imaginary IVs in the kitchen, the living room. I guess I knew then that I was under a spell I had cast myself, an expression born of love and my own suffering. But it was not a choice anymore. It had become something passionately out of my control. The student nurses followed me around. "How do you stay so calm," they asked. I smiled, but it was a smile of desperation. I *needed* to be calm. I *needed* to succeed.

That year I'd found out what nurses really do, and I was going to save the world.

CHAPTER 14

"Dearest Mother, hold me. The pain is so hard to watch. Give me all that I need to heal those in my care."

My first patient to die, Lydia, was the mother of two grown sons who placed a picture of their beautiful mother at her bedside with a mixture of shame and pride, as if they wanted us to know that she hadn't always been like this. The round soft shape, rosy cheeks, and huge smile now belonged to a tiny fragile bird nesting under white sheets. Her husband never stopped crying, so in love was he with the woman in his life. Mrs. Machiavelli had taught her sons to be open and nurturing. They never left her side. The cancer, winning the war, was causing every breath to be painful, in spite of the morphine. Soothing backrubs were not helpful. Even the accidental light brush of fingertips as her pillow was plumped was agony against her skin and brittle bones.

Her room held the unmistakable odor of death. It lingered on my clothes. I could taste it, a pungent warning. I tried to wrench away its eager grip by opening the windows, but the season was uncooperative and snowflakes skipped in and settled on the sill. To add another blanket to those already piled on the tiny and sweet bird would only bring more pain. I dabbed Vaseline on her cracked lips and I hummed a soft song that I loved from church called "Gentle Woman." I did my job, sliding the morphine into her IV as I was ordered, even as her breathing continued to slow knowing that each breath could be her last. When she slipped away it was just after her loving family had gone for supper. They came back to find me waiting for them. No words were spoken. We all just softly cried.

I washed my patient for the final time and rolled her into the "adult-sized" body bag. I had to wrap it around her brittle frame three times before I could tape it closed. I moved her onto the stretcher as though she were made of fine crystal and then headed for the morgue. Between the icy cold and the deep silence of the dead, my arms and legs were instantly covered in goose bumps. It smelled of formaldehyde and I couldn't wait for tonight's hot shower when I got home. When I returned to the floor the new head nurse thrust a chart into my hand, a new patient to admit. The stretcher was turning into the room next to Mrs. Machiavelli's. I shook my head to loosen the web of sadness that had settled inside of me. My patient's family sent me two-dozen long stemmed roses with a card, "Eternally grateful for your loving care," it said.

I told myself to keep going. There was no time to grieve. It was on to the next patient...on to whatever got thrown in my direction. I could do it. I could do it all.

I tried. I often lost my appetite, drank only coffee for days. I locked my keys in my car and forgot appointments. I stayed focused on the floor by taking on too much, addicted, attached like a barnacle to crisis, anything to keep from feeling too much. I rested only fitfully, slept rarely. My sleepwalking continued as I made my rounds through our tiny house on a nightly basis. Shane was amused. I was lonely and exhausted.

I had finished yet one more sixteen-hour shift. It was midnight and snow was falling. The air was so frigid it was hard to breathe. I had completed every task there was to complete, had left no stone unturned in the manner of all good nurses everywhere. I got in my car and turned it on. Shaking from the cold, I waited endless minutes until the heater kicked in before taking off, making my way down the narrow snow-packed streets. The last place I wanted to go was home, to Shane, to my cramped house and another sleepless night. Weaving a path over the ice, I turned my car toward the beach. I could hear the waves and the intermittent blare of the foghorn, but could see nothing through the snow. The losses of my life begged for, demanded, my tears, and I let them flow until all that was left was a deep void of silence. I was shivering uncontrollably. The snow had turned to sleet and mixed with my tears as the sun came up. I crawled into bed twenty minutes later with frozen hands. Shane slept on, unaware that I'd never come home.

  My son was born a year later. I carried him close to my heart, wrapped in a flannel pouch. I nursed him, loving him with a love that I imagined was deep enough to warm the entire earth. He gazed at me; I sung to him. His deep chocolate eyes drew me into a peaceful, milky world. I would never be the same and I thanked God everyday for the chance to mother him. I still worked part time as a nurse, but began to live full-time. With Matthew's sweet downy head in my palm, I knew I had saved my own life—being his mother saved my life. My grief was dissolving, the loneliness left me and I was the luckiest girl in the world.

  I sometimes sat with my mother in her kitchen. We drank coffee out of the same ancient chipped mugs, and I asked questions that I wished she could answer. I shared my baby as a favor to her, but she took to him like he was water and she was dying of thirst. When she held him, I watched her and became the little girl who hadn't wanted to miss a single movement or breath. I wanted to pretend that my mother had looked at me the way she now gazed at Matthew. Had she ever held me close the way she was holding him at her breast? Had she ever looked at me like a long-lost treasure? Did she remember me waiting for her in the kitchen? Did she recall how much I had adored her? I was unable to ask and likely she would not know the answers. It was better to stay at arm's length than to face the pain of hearing the truth that she just didn't remember.

  I recalled the shoebox of my childhood; half filled with bent and crinkled photos. How could half a shoebox contain the lives of four children? It seemed as if every week I had more pictures to put in Matthew's baby album. We were already on our second one and the shelves in my living room had framed shots of every smile, every day trip, and every holiday. The bindings of my Matthew's baby books will split down the middle, I promised myself, too full to contain all the memories of everything he ever said and did. As a man, he will hold these volumes of memories in his lap and know my love.

Matthew's father, disenchanted with the life of a husband and father, started working late. Shane's parents were angry when we told them our plans to move forty-five minutes away to build a new house, but the price was right and the acres of tall pine trees convinced us. We put our house on the market and sold it right away. I was ready to move, but the builder was taking his sweet time and the completion date moved further and further out. Soon it was March 15th. We were supposed to move on April 1st but the house was nowhere near completion. Didn't he understand that I had a child? It seemed not. After one of his particularly pathetic tales of woe about busy schedules and back-ordered materials, I locked myself in the bathroom and let the tears of frustration roll over my cheeks and down my jersey stained with baby fluids. We had outgrown this tiny home. A new home, a bigger and shinier place would heal Shane and I.

I remembered the weekend Shane and I had painted the outside of our little house by ourselves, two full coats in two full days. When Matt was born we gave him the only bedroom and bought a pullout couch for us. We crammed it into the corner of the "Florida" room, which boasted a bar and three stools. When we pulled out the bed, the stools had to be put up against the wall. Shane loved to entertain his friends at the bar. Each morning I woke up with my head an inch from the bar's counter and Shane's favorite sculpture of a black clay hand with the middle finger sticking up. Neon beer signs hung on the back wall and Allman Brothers posters were stuck up with tape anywhere else there was wall space. One day I had forgotten how the room smelled like beer and of the haunting gesture of the artwork—the day when Matthew took his first crawl across the rusty orange carpet in the sunlight, first backward as if working out the kinks, and then forward, off like a shot. Now the tiny home was officially his playground and I loved watching him crawl into the kitchen, emptying the cabinets of all of the Farberware and making music that made him smile.

Interior designing wasn't really my thing, but I had made the effort to surround us with things that were special. I hung fishing net in the corner of the living room and in it I placed all the treasures we found on our trips to the beach. I proudly displayed my crystal glasses with the shamrocks along their gold rims on the mantle. I splurged on Beatrix Potter wallpaper and a matching soft, fuzzy mobile to hang over the crib in Matthew's room. I'd given him my huge teddy bear, the one my father got me when I was only one day old. Shane said the curtains were "too girly," but really he had no say. It was our room, mine and my son's, where we played, snuggled, and loved. Shane's opinion didn't mean much. He loved Matthew but he worried that his fun filled twenty something life was out of his reach. He wasn't as attentive to either one of us. It didn't matter if it was rolling a ball or roughhousing, Shane ran out of patience before Matthew had warmed up to the game. He was more interested in getting to a Blues club in Cambridge with friends or going to the stock car races. We started to argue a lot, especially when he'd go out and leave Matthew with a sitter during the evenings that I worked.

Shane was excited about building the house and I was sure it would bring us closer again. We'd plan it together, I thought, recalling that day we'd painted and he'd dabbed my nose with his brush. Maybe I'd have another baby and we'd be happy. Maybe things would be different then. I could entertain his friends and make my famous potato salad. He could have a pool table in the basement. He could have his workshop for his tools and we agreed that he could have a new truck, too.

The day after we moved out of our sweet tiny home, I stepped back over the threshold with Matthew in my arms to pick up a few things I had forgotten. The new renters were already there. Already there were strange couches and figurines, cigarette butts in the sink, and the rust rug had been torn up. The new home still not ready, we packed up and moved into a trailer in Shane's parents' driveway that brought on a shudder every time I stepped foot inside. For a couple of months after that my aunt's vacated house had been available and we'd lived as transients out of cardboard boxes. Aunt Geraldine had left for her day in the sun, but the realtors, high heels snapping and briefcases swaying, came by every day to show the house. One night Shane, in a fit of frustration put a huge hole in one of the bedroom doors. I don't remember what set him off that time. It didn't take much to make him angry in those days. Maybe we'd run out of toilet paper or he'd hit a snag in fixing his truck radiator, but it didn't really matter. I'd always wanted a nice set of china with lilacs on the edges, but knew I was better off with the cheap stuff, the way he threw dishes across the room when things didn't go his way. My best friend's front porch was our last resort after my aunt's house was sold. Somehow I had patched the hole and I'd hoped it had been overlooked. The only request Susan made was that Shane had to promise not to smoke pot in their house. He didn't even bother to try to comply with that one. I had to work with this friend, a fellow nurse, and the embarrassment was overwhelming.

Finally, after what seemed like years of unsettled days, the house was complete. I avoided the truth of what our marriage had become in favor of paints and rugs and fixtures. I was determined to make us a home and Shane seemed happy with this sprawling brand new raised, ranch, a measure of his success. I'd hoped that he'd love me again.

CHAPTER 15

"Dearest Jesus, I am overwhelmed. I thank you for the beautiful son you have given me. He brings strength, life and joy to me. Bless him every day and guide me always to be a loving and knowing mother."

Though my new home was miles from my mother, our lives were still held tightly together by disappointments and simmering anxieties. She had begun dating and had recently broken up with some man who told her that he was an agent for the CIA. My mother believed it all, as gullible was her middle name. After one of her last dates with 'Hank', I found her covered in bruises.

I couldn't fathom where my mother had dug up this newest guy. Ronald was his name. I should have been happy to hand her over to him, I guess, since nothing had really changed and I'd been permanently on call since I'd left her house. Her calls came regularly, frantic, hysterical, and needing immediate attention. I was the provider of emotional Bandaids, firm lectures, and ultimatums, whatever it took. One day, Shane and I dropped by her house to show her some new pictures of Matthew. My brother and his future wife were sitting on the couch looking startled and worried, alongside Ronald, whose pale face was stricken. One look at my mother told me she was headed for another stay and that I would have to be the one to bring her, kicking and screaming, in the back of Shane's car. I'll bet Ronald hadn't counted on this particular scenario but I'd be rather sure that he had a role in all of it. Shane was always good to my mother and she loved him. Somehow he managed to calm her down and later, going over the day in my mind, I remembered why I loved him.

During the wedding ceremony, nobody gave my mother away. Instead, she gave away my father's remaining life insurance money to her new husband. Ronald paid off his broken-down house with my father's hard-earned cash and then gave another hunk to one of his estranged daughters. They married in the church we grew up in, the church where we buried my father. Ronald's paranoid schizophrenic son sat next to me smelling of bad bologna, his eyes relentlessly boring holes through me. His daughter, dressed in leather and chains, brought her hyperactive son and a box of frosted Rice Krispies to throw at the happy couple.

It was a blissful coming together, the union of drinking partner to a strong sense of false security. Ronald was a security guard. My sister, now in high school, had every freedom. No one paid the slightest mind to her comings and goings. Where she went was a mystery, as were the thoughts she had in her head. She kept the details of this dismal new family to herself, and she made it clear she didn't want my interference or questions. She was out of school more than in it, I knew. Having a good time, I guess. I heard through my brother about a trip she made to Canada one weekend, going to bars at fifteen. She'd told my mother that she was going skiing. Colleen had always hated the snow, but no one noticed.

My mother called me on my birthday. When she wished me well in a thick, slurred voice I put Matthew in the car and took off. I pulled into her driveway and felt myself stiffen. When I opened the door, the familiar sickeningly sweet smell greeted me and I saw her on the floor. Unconscious, full of Valium and beer, my mother lay motionless on the floor. I tripped over her, reaching for the phone to call the ambulance. I was sick. Twenty years, nothing had changed. My mother's husband came in after a hard day of Keno just as I was hanging up and he started slapping my mother's face, trying to wake her. He screamed at me to get off the phone, that she'd be okay. The next few minutes were a blur. He shouted at me, so loud the pain of it tore through my head. He cornered me, in my face, threatening me. From somewhere deep inside, somewhere from under twenty layers, someone who looked like me and sounded like me surfaced to tell this man that if he came any closer I'd kill him. "I'm in charge, now," the voice said, thick with rage, "Things are going to change in this dump." He left before the ambulance arrived, a scratch ticket burning a hole in his pocket.

My mother came home a few days later looking defeated and ashamed. The visiting nurses would come now. For a while, she'd be sober, bathed, and fed. They would watch her when I couldn't. This is how my mother would spend her last few years.

CHAPTER 16

"Dear God, I need help. Please just help me get through, putting one foot in front of the other. Thank you for all that is good."

Shane took a job with a plumbing company closer to the new house, and we suddenly had plenty of money. Matthew, three years old, threw temper tantrums that rivaled his father's. I begged Shane to consider blacktopping what we referred to as a driveway but it was really just an uphill mudslide, a mile long which ran through a sizable chunk of land full of pine trees. He bought a new truck instead. Since it was a standard transmission and I wasn't familiar with using a clutch, I figured out pretty fast that the truck was for him, not "us," as he'd insisted. One night after midnight on my way home from work, I steered into the poorly lit drive. It was dark and cold and I was beyond tired. I felt my hatchback Pinto swerve into one of the muddy ruts that were hard to avoid as I tried to make my way up the incline before the car's transmission gave out altogether. No such luck. I swore and got out, put my shoes down into the mud. I walked up to the house, swearing the whole way, and let myself in the door. My white stockings and white clogs were caked with dirt and pine needles. I stopped in my tracks and took stock of the situation. Was all this money we made for our family...for me and for Matthew...or for Shane, for partying with his friends? Then I asked myself what I had not dared until tonight, not even in the privacy of my own thoughts. Where were all the hundreds of dollars coming from...the rolled bills in his suit-coat pockets, stuffed to the back of dresser drawers, shoved under the eaves in the attic? Within a year, I would learn that Shane was hiding too much and the fighting about it became too much. We spent a few months in counseling together but good changes were not coming.

I pushed my clothes down into the washing machine and scraped the mud from my shoes as best I could. I willed myself to look back at the six years of selfishness, fits of temper, and deceit, and I knew my life had to change.

I collapsed into bed, hugging the edge as if my life depended on it. Shane, sound asleep, heard nothing. The next day, feeling like a failure and almost changing my mind, I told Shane that I wanted a divorce. In his fury, he hurled the last thing he would throw in my house and I found the strength to stand by my decision. And I knew that I would always love the part of us that brought Matthew to the world.

I chose a warm summer night to be the last in my dream house. Matthew still fast asleep, I went outside and spread a blanket. Under the full moon I let myself cry, just me and the white pines. *Do it*, they whispered. I loved them; I'd miss falling asleep to their sound outside my bedroom window. This huge yard had seen the beginnings of my little boy's adventures. "I'm searching for clues, Mamma," he told me, wandering just far enough to state his independence, staying just close enough to feel the reach of my heart. Thick beads of sap fell into his hair and "sticky birds" attached themselves to his Osh-Kosh overalls as he collected creatures—anything small enough to fit into his glass jar. I'd lost the battle long ago to keep him clean. He was happiest dirty, which was as it should be, and he got into everything. "Doggie," stuffed dog extraordinaire, was hooked into his belt loop for hands-free maneuverability. Doggie missed not one ride in Matthew's car seat on the way to preschool and stayed buckled in all day until Matthew's return. Moving to the city would bring me closer to work but further away from the pure fresh-air days I cherished. The row house I'd bought for us had no yard, but Quincy was where I'd grown up and I was hoping for that reason alone it might feel like home. I planned to bring Matthew to the beach and to the local playground as often as I could.

I looked down at my child, sleeping peacefully with Doggie held tightly in his arms. His forehead was damp and his eyelids twitched with dreams of captive crickets and frogs. I stroked his arm gently, not wanting to wake him. I told myself that I would succeed at my new job and that Matthew would go to kindergarten; that it would be okay. That it had to be okay.

In the morning, I took one last look around at the paint, the furniture, and the trappings of happiness. Everything we needed fit in the back seat of the car, there was nothing else to keep me. I picked up Matthew and Doggie and closed the door. I swore I'd never look back.

I had never really been on my own before, and the doubts began creeping in before I made it down the "driveway." I was afraid. What did I think I was doing, choosing to be responsible for Matthew alone, in a strange place? His father had agreed to an every-other-weekend arrangement. I told him he could see Matt as often as he wanted, but I guess four days a month was okay with him. How would I manage a house myself? I was terrified and my feelings of failure about hurting Shane and his parents would paralyze me from time to time. One of the worst mornings of my life was coming down the courthouse steps to say goodbye to the man I thought I'd grow old with.

We drove up to the clapboard building sandwiched into between two other identical ones at about noon and used the rest of the day to unpack. Matt was overtired and by the time we ate dinner, macaroni and cheese out of the box, he was throwing his food. When I finally got him to settle down for the night, I collapsed myself and looked around. Not quite what I'd planned for myself or for my firstborn, but it would have to do. I went back upstairs to check on Matt, spent a couple of minutes listening to him breathe, and then went downstairs to check the locks again before heading for bed myself. I needed some rest.

The screaming began as I got into bed. Twelve minutes later the neighbor on the other side of the wall was carried out, arms and legs flailing, to be loaded onto an ambulance. Through the window I caught snatches of "back to the funny farm," from the family next door. It hit all too close to home for my taste, and I was glad Matthew had slept through it.

The next night, the Millers, neighbors to my left this time, let me know they had "plumbing problems" after the remnants of their spaghetti supper backed up into my kitchen sink. The neighbors across the street weren't much better, six college guys trying to peak into my windows. I made a snap decision. Who needed curtains when blankets and tacks would do just fine.

I sat behind a desk at my new job and considered my future. With eight hours a day sitting reviewing medical claims, things didn't look too hopeful. My business cards said I was a "utilization review specialist"—whatever that meant. I had no idea what I was doing. All I knew was that just getting by was the only thing that came naturally these days.

Nine hours later I stood up and stretched, relieved to be leaving, but grateful for the normal hours with weekends and holidays off, like other normal people. It was a tradeoff. I got to stay behind the desk as Matthew was picked up from school each day and brought to the YMCA for an after-school program. I pictured him getting off the bus at the Y. I added a smile on his face but I knew a scowl was more likely. We were trying to adjust, he and I, and it wasn't easy. "It's better than going home to a babysitter, isn't it?" I said each morning, but from the daggers in his eyes I don't think he got my point. What I didn't say but thought with equal amounts of relief and guilt was that child support paid for it. Of course, that meant it paid for nothing else, with nothing left over. I looked forward to letting Matthew play with the other neighborhood kids after supper.

Though I sat all day, I was tired when I got home. After another meal of pasta (Matt was in a phase where he'd eat only white foods), I put my feet up on the coffee table and waited for my nightly fix of *Jeopardy*. I leaned back on the couch and closed my eyes. I'd take just a moment, and then go check on Matthew. I had just started to drift off with the spring breeze on my face when a pounding at the door startled me awake. I bolted upright and shook the fuzziness away. A woman was on the stoop; I could see her through the narrow window by the door. They're to welcome us to the neighborhood? Pleased, I combed my fingers through my hair and answered the door with my nicest first-impression smile. The woman, in a perfect pageboy and impeccable pale blue business suit, held a knife in her hands. I stared at it, confused. "Are you aware," she said, "that your son took this out to play?" Her voice was shrill and cut as sharply as the blade in her hands. It was a large carving knife, my best one. Dumbfounded, I could find no words. "Did you hear what I said?" she demanded. "Your son took this outside to play!" I finally found my tongue and sputtered an apology. I apologized over and over and over again to her face and then to her back as she stomped away from me, clearly unimpressed. "MATTHEW," I yelled with as much fear-inducing mother power as I had, "Get in the house...NOW!" I have to admit it was satisfying—and a relief—when Matthew responded in seconds to the blood-curdling call. He was in bed within the hour. We'd been officially welcomed to the neighborhood.

Days turned into months of routine, out by seven-thirty in the morning and back by six at night. I was tired all of the time. Domino's pizza knew our order and address. We were now on a first-name basis with Bart, Jason, and Peter, the delivery boys. I remembered a time when I'd loved to cook, but all I felt lately was compressed, as though someone were sitting on my shoulders. I had looked forward to walking to and from my office, but every step was an effort, especially in high heels. I felt lost, clicking down the street in shoes that were the only real thing about me. No, that wasn't right either. I was a professional. I was put together. *I'm a mess.* The thoughts played over and over in my head, keeping time with my footfalls, *I'll step out of my shoes...I'll run away...I'll never come back.*

I sat at my desk and long minutes ticked by while I pictured my favorite black patent leather heels, one upright and one turned on its side, alone on the concrete sidewalk after I'd made my getaway. I never knew that depression crept, that it was a sneaky, menacing thing. I knew now that it had been following me like a dark shadow, a cloudy slithering shadow with a far reach. Each time I turned around, it had ducked away to hide...had vanished...until one day it climbed into my back pocket to stay.

It enveloped me. First came the hopelessness and then I couldn't get out of bed. It held me so tight I could hardly breathe. But it was better than not being held at all, wasn't it? I congratulated myself at the thought. I must be okay if I was still making jokes, right? But it was a sick comfort, a peace pipe offered up to the god of depression, which only held sway as long as I dragged myself out of bed and went to work. Then one day I didn't get up at all. When Matthew came to my bedside and whined, I told him to get his own breakfast and get himself off to school. That was the day of his teddy bear picnic, he reminded me. I'd put a sticker on the calendar and written TEDDY BEAR PICNIC – 1 PM!!! But I had forgotten. I hadn't looked at the calendar in weeks. I blew him a kiss, told him I'd see him later, and went back to sleep. I slept through the morning, and then lunch. I slept right through the picnic. I never knew I hadn't shown up. I was oblivious.

It was hard looking into Matthew's accusing eyes when he got off the bus at the end of the day. I heard the frustration and anger in his voice, teetering on tears, "Where were you,

Mom, I waited for you." At that moment I realized I'd only been familiar with self-hatred, only skimmed its surface, having worn its skin for some time, but I'd never hated myself like this, so much, with such venom. "I don't know, Matthew, I don't know." How could I not know? How could I have known this kind of pain myself and then willingly put it at my son's doorstep? He put his arms around my neck, loving me still. How could he love me so? I wished for it to be yesterday all over again so that I could do it right. I didn't deserve the love I saw in his deep chocolate eyes.

That night, after pizza, I made a call. On the phone with her, I could only say, "I'm sad, I'm a mother, and I need help."

Rachel saw me the very next day. Her couch reminded me of the one in our cellar while I was growing up, well worn, with holes in it. I snuggled up on it late at night and watched the mummy movies, scared to death. Rachel was warm and I trusted her. But I *had* to, I was out of options. I heard her ask me if I had thoughts of suicide and I was shocked—not that she'd asked, but that the answer was still no. "No," I told her, "but I did lots of times when I was growing up." Hearing this, she settled back in her brown tweed chair that bobbed a little each time she nodded her head. I watched as she folded her hands and crossed her legs at the ankle. Her shoes were frayed and scuffed and out of style, like her dress. It pleased me to think she was too busy to shop, too busy thinking of others, and too busy putting herself last. Her hair was curly and soft looking. I always wanted to have wash-and-wear hair like that. Rachel wore no makeup and I liked that too. She was real, not made up, and she looked at me as though she had loved me my whole life. I saw her lips form the words, "Think of this time as your time, Kate. Think of this room as your safe place. Dump it all here, I'm with you," but it took a few moments for the meaning to catch up in my head.

Rachel held me in her arms in her drab but comfortable office two days a week on my lunch hour. I didn't want to be any later than I had to for Matthew so giving up my lunch hours was a small price to pay. I saw myself as Humpty Dumpty, somehow managing to glue the pieces back together and climb back up on the wall of my life. I drove to work with the mascara brush in one hand, cover-up in the other, praying the tracks of my tears were evident only to me. I felt like an old woman carrying an old carpetbag filled with a very heavy life— my very heavy life. Two days a week we emptied the bag, bit by bit. When will it get easier to carry, I asked Rachel? I cried like a child, skinning my knees under Rachel's careful watch. Finding the courage and the words was like pulling off a huge Bandaid—excruciatingly slow, taking the skin with it. I was an endless source of tears. I sat on her tattered couch with all of my stuffing hanging out while pieces of me raged all over the room. I felt each and every piece, jagged and sharp, as it hit the walls and ceiling. I cried for the childhood I never had. I wanted to throw up, to purge myself of the layers of losses, and the lost layers of the life that was mine. I was a collection of raw fragments picking my way through a minefield of sharp shards of myself. Rachel picked them up, one by one, when it was time to leave, always allowing me an extra minute to gather my wits about me, always knowing how much I needed the time. My feet knew the way to the door by now. On autopilot, I turned the knob, not brave enough to look back, even after so many sessions. "You'll be alright, Kate, you'll be alright," Rachel called out, each and every time, and I listened for the echoes all the way down the hall, wishing I could take them with me out into the world.

  How long could it go on—this spilling of guts, this convulsing need to purge what had been and what I needed but would never be. Weeks...months...years? Would I learn to forgive my mother for her absences? My father for his? Could I ever forgive myself for not taking care of myself, pulling at my hair, ignoring the pain? And more than that, could I ever stop thinking of hating my mother during her illnesses, times when she couldn't get out of bed, never mind even considering going to or missing a teddy bear picnic. The nuns had advocated forgiveness. But I knew forgiveness took time, at least the kind of forgiveness I was searching for. Forgiving in a convent was easy. In life? Not so much.

Rachel held my hand as we dove again and again into the painful, frigid, churning waters of my past; only I was so afraid I would never make it out. "Where's my lifeline," I demanded to know. "Where's the branch? There's no oar, not even a pathetic piece of driftwood floating my way. Please, I need to know, where's my lifeline? I need a lifeline." And Rachel's hand would hold tight to mine. I was terrified of being my mother.

It didn't have to be that way, it shouldn't have been that way, but it was, it was. I hated them. I loved them, but I hated them. I hurt too much.

"I'm so sad, Rachel, so very sad."

"Of course you are."

"I'm broken."

"But soon you'll be whole."

Rachel did not stop holding me and neither did the Blessed Mother. I continued to go for weekly sessions for a long time, ever so slowly beginning to feel my head above water. Then one day I looked up and there was Richard. Richard came into my life summoned by some force of grace. I took everything he offered as it came my way. I hadn't even known to look for it, let alone what form it might take. He'd loved me for a long time, he said. A long time? I thought blankly. I had first noticed him the day I watched him clean the snow from my windshield in the parking lot at work. I was irritated. What did he think he was doing? I thought about yelling out the window for him to stop, that I didn't know him, that it wasn't right.

Richard was saying he worked in the building beside mine. I shook my head to rejoin the present. "I see you walk to lunch everyday," he said. "Someone so pretty should be smiling." He made me smile when he said that and soon he was making me bread, feeding me. I was the small bird he nourished slowly and carefully with a dropper full of whatever he thought I needed. I tried to give back, it was only fair, but he persisted. "No, no, it's okay, not now." He read to Matthew, played catch with him and took him to museums. When Matthew was asleep, he led me to the tub where he bathed me and washed my hair. In bed, I lay on his chest and slept better than I had in years. He sang to me in the morning, my favorite, *Moon River*.

Come spring, I was the first crocus poking through the earth, surviving those first frosty springtime nights without a hitch. Just when you thought winter would never end, up through the last traces of snow came the earthy reminders that life would go on. I was right on time. I was whole. I was a Utilization Review Specialist and had my own box of business cards to prove it. I could be strong. I would be stronger than ever before. I knew that now and in knowing this, I came back. When I surfaced I remembered knowing what I had known all along but forgotten, that I had never been alone.

Matthew was waiting patiently for me the way he did every night, his hair a ruffled mess and his eyes tired but happy. I often picked him up from the YMCA and drove us to the beach to have dinner on our favorite blanket before doing all the things we loved to do, skimming rocks, finding shells, precious Mother and son time. Home again, we read *The Little Engine That Could* until his eyes blurred over, melted with sleepy love. Next to my bed I found the first flowers of my first spring, pinched way too close and leaving hardly any stem, stuffed into a jelly jar. *Love, Matthew.*

My Richard moved away when I declined to make him my husband. I had grown accustomed to his warmth and his caring, but the bridge I needed to link me to life had become a bridge I needed to cross alone. I wanted him to understand. "I just can't right now," I told him.

"But I can't wait," he said.

CHAPTER 17

"Dear Mary, sometimes I find myself forgetting to pray and yet it's just what I need to do.

I knelt down on the hideous rug in my new bedroom. The springtime evening sun was setting and the room was aglow. Please remind me of all that I need to know and come to me when I most need it."

  I stayed lost under a pile of claim forms for a while, but I missed the ward. Out came my pristine whites from the back of the closet and in days I was employed at the local hospital where I needed to be, with people who needed what I had to offer. Life went on. My sweet Matthew's happiness mirrored my own. His energy, boundlessly exuberant, carried through school, play, dinner, and a bath he "didn't need," after which he fell into my arms, a balloon with no air left inside to hold it up. The neighborhood had looked forward to a bigger stir than we actually created based on the knife incident. Now all was forgotten in the interests of getting along and we began to find our place amongst the students, families, and local storefronts.

  I attacked the house with a new vigor, ripping up rugs, pulling down old paneling, painting. It was time to move on and move in, not just with boxes but also with intent. I was experiencing the pride of accomplishment, letting go of my feelings of failure and moving on. In just a fleeting moment of guilt, my old diamond ring bought new curtains. I found a print of the Boston Common that reminded me of walks with my grandmother. The shells that Matthew and I found were cherished pieces on a new coffee table. I handled the starlings that came through the dryer vent into my basement with Tipi Hendren ease. I bought cut flowers whenever I had an extra few dollars. I made cookies for Matthew and his friends and I grounded him swiftly for the time he rode his bike too far from home. I found him on a very busy section of Southern Artery in Quincy, his bike parked outside a Dunkin' Donuts.

My brother, Colin called and said he had a friend who was interested in me but Matthew and I were living our lives and the lack of drama felt good. The weekends when Shane took Matthew were long and sometimes lonely.

It was already late spring before I decided to pick up the phone and call Declan. When he didn't answer I left a nervous high-pitched message on his machine and hung up feeling the old fire on my neck and face. I was sure he'd sense my discomfort and tell Colin his sister was a loser. But he called the next day, seemingly not put off by my lack of social skills. A couple of days later he came to the door holding a violet plant in his big hands, looking for all the world like a kid bringing an apple to the teacher. We were going for a bike ride to Wollaston Beach and then to the Clam Box. I'd been looking forward to it in a jittery sort of way but already I was cursing my own vanity for squeezing myself into a new pair of size four *Guess* jeans just because I was so thrilled they fit. I knew I'd pay sorely by the time we got there.

Biking made conversation sporadic and gave me a chance to get my bearings. By the time we faced plates piled high with fried clams and tartar sauce and French fries the size of Rhode Island, I was doing what I always did on dates: listening. In my experience, which was admittedly somewhat limited, men never quite noticed if they did all the talking. Declan was full of stories and I listened, sitting primly, smiling sweetly, nodding from time to time in encouragement. It worked like a charm, as it always had before. Declan liked me. He made it a point though to crane his neck to look at any female walking by. He always did that and always would. Why do some men think they need to make sure that you don't think you're too special? Of course, he was a handsome young man and by this time, I was feeling pretty insecure. We started to date officially. On our third date to see the Newport mansions Declan locked himself out of his condo with his car keys inside. (He'd always do that kind of thing, too.) We went around back to his terrace where he threw off his shirt and climbed up to let himself in through the sliding glass doors of his balcony. Tracking the lithe movements of his young, strong back and arms, I felt a stirring I hadn't felt in years. That night in the light of a gigantic full moon, we made love and he said I was the most beautiful woman he had ever seen.

The day Declan moved in with Matthew and me, I told him outright that we were perfectly capable of supporting ourselves, that he wasn't there to support us. Independence was important to me and I wasn't willing to give it up, not yet. I told myself that he appreciated my backbone, that he understood who I was. I fed him, sheltered him, washed his clothes, made love to him, and created a family around him. Surely with all that effort he would see what he had in me, a woman who could make him happy.

As an accountant with a steady job, Declan's salary was considerable. He wore nice suits and expensive ties with which I gladly made twice-weekly trips to the dry cleaners, and wing-tipped shoes that needed weekly polishing, a task of domesticity I took on with enthusiasm. I was proud of this good man, this young executive. Except for Declan's unaccountable sporadic moodiness, I was on solid ground.

Declan confessed he was bored with accounting, that he'd like to go to graduate school. Ah, I thought, relieved, that's where the mood swings were coming from. Job boredom I could handle. I was doing everything I could to make him happy and had been anxious that it wasn't enough. I was too afraid to say anything. His sisters were reassuring. It was "all the change," they said, including our marriage plans. "Too much too soon," I overheard one say when I left the room. "It's the *depression*," answered the other meaningfully in a loud whisper. "You know

Declan...he's always been depressed." I acted as if I hadn't heard a word, but inside my stomach was churning with denial.

We talked of marriage long before Declan proposed. One night I came home to a pair of huge new stereo speakers in the living room. "I got a great deal on them," said Declan. "I couldn't resist." He'd used the money he'd been saving for a diamond engagement ring. I looked at him, waiting for the other shoe to drop. It only took a moment. "And, you know what, Kate? I've made my decision. I'm going to quit my job and go back to school. I want to be a history professor."

His Brooks Brothers suits regaled to the closet, I worried that he was just another young, aimless young man. So I did what had to be done. I turned up the oven. I made ultimatums. And sure enough, a poignant few ultimatums later, Declan decided that he had a purpose and that he knew what he wanted. He led me through the woods to a rocky clearing overlooking Nantasket Bay and knelt on one knee. He told me that I had the biggest heart of anyone he'd ever met. "Will you be my wife, Kate?" he said. I loved him during that sunset more than I had loved anyone.

Since that night, and every night since then, a piece of that big heart wishes it had found enough love to say, *Go find your own dream. I don't want to be anyone's purpose.*

The gray days of our early marriage rolled by, some bright and promising moments and then too much loneliness. I was full of guilt over Declan's consuming and unrelenting unhappiness. *I'll make it right*, I promised myself, it's up to me. I pushed my resentments down deep and deeper, until they settled in comfortably with all the others, which resided there together. We worked, we played, and we did what we were supposed to do. I knew Declan loved me, and happiness was not guaranteed.

CHAPTER 18

"I don't want the world, Jesus. I'm so grateful for all that I have. I pray that all will work out but I think I'll have to hand Declan off to you for a while. Could you help him to know that you're there for him? Would you help him to see the bright side of things?"

The fall morning was crisp and clear. I saw puffs of air each time I panted, each labor pain worse than the one before. Declan drove to the hospital with slippers still on his feet. When the time finally arrived, he and I held each other to birth our son. Writhing in pain, I knew joy unlike any other. The doctor yelled out, "Well, if this face doesn't belong to a boy...!" and held out a tiny slippery, bloody head. Declan's cries mingled with the baby's.

Then I looked into my son's eyes and I reasoned that this was our purpose; this was why, the good we were supposed to create. Andrew was an angel, a sturdy kicking reminder that there were all kinds of love and all kinds of beautiful miracles. I nuzzled my baby's neck, pausing only to fill baby books, and life went on for Declan and me. Andrew, with his surprising chuckle so early in life, made the sun come out every day. His father loved him with intensity that I was grateful to be a part of. I loved Declan all the more for that. Matthew, eight years older than his brother, was busy with his life, stopping always to give Andrew a quick kiss on his head. I continued to work as a nurse part time, enjoying my boys and my home.

My husband's depressions continued and finally he sought clinical help. It was a fight to get him to agree and often I felt exhausted by the struggle. It was all so reminiscent of my years with my mother and even at this time, I was still the one called on if she became ill again. Financial problems were also overwhelming as Declan changed jobs. He had always been a hard worker keeping late hours often. He felt tired from this and assumed that a change in career would do him good. He never did go back to school to become a history professor. I felt guilt for that but inside I knew that his depression, unless fully treated, would follow him wherever he would go.

He took a job doing sales, a complete change from anything he'd ever done but which required people skills and energy that he couldn't find at that time. I worked extra hours and took home paperwork that my home care agency would pay me to do. Time passed and things improved. Declan found another good job, one in which he was quite qualified for and the feelings of success helped us all. We found more happiness as a young family, less financial worry and I was able to work less and focus on graduate school. Soon after, I found myself pregnant and though I worried of the timing in our lives, I welcomed the feeling of new life.

I had managed to crawl back into bed with yet one more bowl of strawberries, my most recent insatiable craving, and was shifting around trying to get comfortable. Nine months pregnant and counting. As the bowl lifted and fell in waves activated by my daughter-to-be, I was thinking about how I had changed, how my thoughts were ebbing and flowing with the undulations of my body. There had been nothing else for weeks. My shape, so transformed, so unique, captured my every waking moment. The shape of everything in my world had shifted and I reveled in my own gift to myself, a womb of comfort and care. I never felt more of a woman than when I carried this child, dressed in my favorite black mini-dress that clung to every curve, accentuating the roundness of the feminine life within me. I was aroused around the clock. I grew my hair long and wore dangling earrings. I felt a change in me, from a young female to a full and strong woman. It was that simple. Only the sleepless nights, rolling over and back again with an aching back and a constantly full bladder, kept me from wishing it would last forever. They told me my daughter was planning on coming into the world feet first. I lay down on an ironing board and held headphones playing *Les Miserables* to my belly, coaxing her to turn. I sang songs to her as I readied her room, hoping she'd remember the melodies when I finally got the chance to hold her and we danced together in the starlight.

I put down the half-full bowl of berries and turned off the light. I was hoping for at least a couple hours of sleep. After an hour of discomfort, however, I knew it was not to be. *"Declan!"* Exhilarated, I was laughing and crying. *"She's coming!"* I took slow breaths. I would not be rushed. I reached for my brush and made long, slow strokes through my thick hair. Kathryn and I would soon be two, face to face, side by side. I prayed to Mary. *Please let me be a good mother to her.* The pain sent me reeling and I wrapped my arms around my belly with tears and gratitude.

Suddenly the phone on the night table next to the bed rang out, disturbing me, disturbing the moment. "Is this Kate Russell? This is the Jordan Hospital calling. Can you come pick up your mother and bring her home as soon as possible? She's in the E.R."

Pant-pant. "What? Who is this?"

"It's Jordan Hospital," the voice said again, more slowly. The person sounded annoyed, as if she were speaking to someone of lesser intelligence. "It's your mother. She came in an hour ago."

"My mother?" I panted some more. An hour ago? Her heart?

"What is it?" Declan whispered, "Her heart?"

He took the phone from my hand. "This is her son-in-law. What's going on? Is it her heart? Oh, oh, I see."

111

Declan's face had taken on a clinched look. "No, no, I understand. Yes, I'll tell her."

I didn't want to hear. *I was having a baby!*

Declan looked at me and then away. "She's just drunk," he said. "They examined her. There's nothing wrong." He waited for me to respond, not sure what to do.

I panted in and out a couple of times before answering, before screaming into the phone, "Tell them to call her a cab ride home!"

How dare she intrude on this night? How dare she?

Declan was pacing around the bedroom, nervous and picking his fingers. I knew he would be uncomfortable again with my standing up for myself. I sat consumed by anger, watching him grind strawberry juice into the carpet, staining it a deep wounded red. Red with the anger I had toward my mother. Red with the resentment I had toward this man who had never understood what I felt about my mother and what I needed from him even though I shared everything with him. My anger was palpable...a living, breathing thing that unsettled him as it always did. It didn't matter what kind it was. There were all kinds. Anger born of frustration. Angry silences of rejection. Anger that he wasn't living up to my expectations. But I wanted to be angry. I wanted to show my anger and live my anger, give it life, not control it for his sake. And then let it go away, leaving me healthier for trying not to stuff down my feelings any longer.

We called the sitter, who came over to spend the night with the kids, then got into the car and made the short trip to the hospital in silence. When my only daughter was born forgiveness was still something out of my reach.

It had taken over twelve hours on all fours on the floor to give birth to my daughter as women have done since the beginning of time. But I had the sense that I had done something brand new. I was immense, magnificent with the rush of power. I pushed her out with a reservoir of endurance and strength I had no idea I was capable of. Declan caught our baby in a strong and capable grasp. I loved the strength and quickness of his hands in that triumphant moment and it was a moment that was new and foreign to him and yet spirit moved him toward his purpose. Our daughter was born to screams of joy and delight, like a surprise birthday party for a very important person. A world of midwives greeted her and her smiling father, a hero in a moment of complete love and forgiveness, put Kathryn on my bare chest. I looked quickly at him, remembering why I loved him and then held my girl.

She stared at me, wet and bloody, warm as my insides. Green eyes...we both had green eyes. "Welcome," I whispered. "I'm your mother, and I will love you forever."

CHAPTER 19

"Jesus, reach for me. Spirit, strengthen me. God, catch me."

Two weeks later my mother lay motionless after a stroke. A similar call had come in the night, but this time her drinking had taken second place. I spoke for her and stayed by her side.

Only fifty-six years old, she was too young for Medicare...too young for *this*. She went home again with a team of visiting nurses. She was weak on one side and fell if unsupported. Her thinking was fuzzy, her judgment not the best. My mother was poor; her home, falling apart, mirrored her health. Our high school pictures, lined up on her faux marble mantle, faced the hospital bed now set up in the middle of her living room. The walls were thickly coated in a yellow smoky resin; the window glass was covered in a dirty film, which had obscured the light of day for years. I idly wondered if they'd ever been washed. I looked around some more, poking about, searching for signs of life. She had nothing. The Sacred Heart statue was still missing its hand after the altercation between my mother's second husband and me.

The visiting nurses and the social worker were kind to my mother, experts in not judging, overlooking. After a few more small strokes over the next few months, her speech slowed. She sounded drunk even though she was not, when now it was due only to fatigue. Ronald made himself noticeably scarce. Every day a van picked her up and brought her to a day care facility for the mentally ill.

Surprisingly, my mother rallied. They recruited her to answer the phones, slurred speech and all.

Suddenly everyone loved *Joanie*. My mother, in her pathetic state, had finally found success as a receptionist. She never missed a day of work, not wanting to disappoint, not letting on when she didn't feel well, bound and determined to be there for them. "There are always those worse off," she told me, chipper in a way I'd never heard before. Younger patients asked for her advice; others wanted her friendship. Soon I hardly heard from her anymore, so needed now and so giving to her new family. When the center was closed, I made weekend visits with three children in tow to her house. I didn't want to go and argued with myself every time, but knew I would capitulate. I shouldn't stay away. I couldn't stay away.

On one of those visits I opened her door, as always wishing I were somewhere else, anywhere else, to find her expression had changed. A lopsided smile filled her face with warmth that stirred me. Immediately I resented my reaction and her ability to stir me, both. Always so vulnerable in my eyes, today she appeared whole. She looked as though she had an answer for everything, a calmness, a knowing. I had trouble breathing and I felt unbalanced. I put Kathryn down on the dirty rug and stared at my mother. I sat down next to her, almost reaching out to touch her. We looked at each other for so long in the peaceful silence. I looked at my mother for so long and with such growing tenderness that I never noticed that my baby daughter sat upright for the first time.

The youngest of seven children, my mother was the baby no one had time for. The death of the oldest, the pilot shot down in World War II, had left Nana in a permanent state of mourning. Pasty, half dead, Nana rocked in her chair by the window in her apron, feeling nothing. She watched the skies as if Buddy's plane would be flying overhead, landing in the back yard. I thought of her briefly as I watched my mother and a new compassion grew within me for her, as well. When my grandfather retired he hid in the basement, grateful for the lack of scolding, drinking as much as he wanted. So, my mother had lost her father, too. Since they hadn't liked my own father (with his quarter-German heritage) and clearly had no use for us, I assumed their antipathy had carried over to us kids. I remembered this now as I looked at my mother, catching heartfelt snapshots of her as a baby and then as a young girl.

I saw her as a teenager fighting with her father, crying over a boy. I saw her falling in love. I felt the hope she must have had as a young bride and mother. In her presence that day, I appreciated her perfume, very light and sweet. I felt tears stinging when I noticed her lipstick, a flattering soft pink. I had in that moment, the grace of knowing how life had been for her. I understood with deep loving clarity that she had wanted things to be different. As my baby daughter delighted herself with her newfound posture, I reached to my mother. Wells of empathy told me the story she had never spoken about, how it was for her, how sometimes getting out of bed was like climbing Mount Everest; that sometimes she wanted to walk right out of her shoes and run away from everything.

I spotted the black and white crinkled photo that had sat on a dusty table at Nana's house. My mother as a young girl was standing alone and off to the side, as though the photographer didn't know how to focus on his subject. She's a shadow of herself, in camouflage against a nondescript background. My chest tightened. I knew with complete certainty all the ways that her own mother had let her down. My mother, endlessly trying to get Nana's attention, went unnoticed. My mother, eight years old, maybe younger, telling her mother about the neighbor who was "touching" her, and hearing only in response, "Don't tell lies, child. Don't be a liar."

In the morning light, my mother looked ten years older than her age. Unbidden, the telephone company's annual publication came to mind. She still kept it in her hope chest as a reminder that they'd asked her to model swimsuits. I knew she had been a beautiful woman before the years of not coping had caught up with her and had left her looking like someone else.

I saw her when my father died, too broken and too hurt to help her own children, saying goodbye to the only man she had ever loved. I saw it all, scene after scene, frame after frame, like a movie in my head. When she reached out to hold my baby daughter with her shaking hands I hesitated, but only for a moment. I knew no harm would come to my girl.

With a shock of pure physical recognition, I watched as she gazed at my daughter, the way she must surely have once gazed at me. As she tenderly cupped her hand around Kathryn's head and held her to her heart, I felt each stroke on the back of my own head, and my hand floated up by a force of its own. I watched, aching with need. The rare times she had mothered me instantly flooded my senses and filled my heart. Her palm on my forehead, checking for fever. Christmas, when she took out the manger, but said that the baby Jesus had to wait until Christmas Eve. Christmas morning, kneeling and praying before the presents could be opened and then heading for church—with or without her, mostly without—but knowing she was there if only in spirit. The thoughts of her finally freed from judgment. Speaking to me of God, teaching me which saints to pray to and for what, my mother led me.

It was my mother who taught me how to pray and I had learned well.

I prayed all of the time, at school and at my desk, thinking not of math but of getting home to her. Prayers of hope, love, devotion; prayers for her, prayers for me. And I was still praying.

Even now I knew it was St. Anthony who found my keys and the occasional perfect parking space. And she taught me to keep praying most often when you felt you just couldn't bear anymore.

My mother's faith this day was strong. She talked to me of "her God," as if He belonged to her and she to Him. She told me in speech that was slurred and painfully slow that she had had a blessed life.

It is then that I felt honored to have mothered her.

CHAPTER 20

"Holy Mary, Mother of God, pray for us sinners, now and at the hour of our death. Amen."

My mother was taken to the hospital after complications related to heart surgery weeks before. She had not improved. The doctors had called in the middle of the night to ask me what my mother's wishes were regarding end of life. I needed to see her for myself and they assured me that they would do everything possible until I arrived. It was clear that my mother would not survive but she pleaded with me with her blue eyes before she slipped into a coma. I called my sister, Colleen. She was also a nurse and we stayed with my mother. The nurses and the doctors offered to move my mother to a small private room nearby so that we could stay close. She had bled into her brain and there was not anything that could be done and I couldn't forget her eyes.

It took eight hours for my mother to die. Eight hours of my holding her fleshy arm while my life with her traveled through my mind. The room had gone from light to dark during this time, a time when I wanted her suffering to be over but a time when I needed her to stay forever.

When she took her last breath, I shook when I realized that I had screamed, "No, Mom, please Mom, no!" aloud.

Pulling out of the hospital parking lot, I called Declan to say that I was on my way home. "It's all over," I said. "She's gone." I know he was gentle, but I absorbed nothing of what he said. I cranked up the radio, opened the windows, and mindlessly drove through Harvard Square toward home. There were hundreds of people crossing the street, shopping, buying newspapers. Not one of them knew what I had lost. I let the tears fall, wiping them away as furiously as they fell, worrying that I'd hit one of the passersby having just another day.

I wasn't sleeping well. Sometimes when I cried it sounded like it was coming from someone else. The noises come from the deepest of places, unrecognizable to me. I was left in an exhausted heap and had to nap for hours. Her funeral Mass was a beautiful tribute to her and the priest read my words to the crowd. There were so many there from the mental health clinic where she answered phones. It was easy to spot those who had such troubles but the grief was universal. A few weeks later, I forced myself to go through my mother's dresser drawers. I was looking once more for something to keep—anything—as a reminder, a token of her love. I'd been through all but one. About to give up, I made a final swipe with my hand along the side of the drawer and then the back, letting my fingers trace the few cheap mismatched earrings and stained handkerchiefs until the edge of a piece of cardboard stopped my progress. Carefully I drew out a yellowed, creased piece of parchment. On one side was a prayer to the Blessed Mother, the Memorare. She had written in pencil, "never known to fail." On the other side was an imprint of my mother's lips. It was the one she took with her in her vinyl suitcase when she went away, the one I always imagined she clutched in her hands to ease her pain. It always came back with her. I knew it was what led her home, led her back to me.

I saw it and knew then that it had been there all along, waiting for me to claim it. She had saved it and I had found it. It was my connection to her, and to everything else. I held it tightly in my hands.

CHAPTER 21

"Dearest St. Jude, thank you for answered prayers. Please hold the hands of anyone who worries about hopelessness. Please give them all of the faith they need, through the intercession of Jesus and his most holy and beautiful mother."

Tomorrow is the first day of school. Kathryn and I sit in the warm kitchen with sunlight pouring through the sheer curtains that frame the soft floral wallpaper. We trade stories of the best days of this last summer, officially over at the end of the day. We sip lemonade, leaning on the sturdy oak table. Kathryn wistfully announces that there are only one hundred eighty more days until next summer and listens with half an ear, to my pep talk about new beginnings. Andrew says he's going to wear shorts until the first snow. When Kathryn laughs, he protests. I listen to my children teasing each other and silently vow to find a few more days at the beach, alone, with my writing. But not yet, I don't want the end of summer either. My beautiful children's freckled faces search mine, waiting. They know what's coming. It's time for the annual Big Plan, every year on the last day of their vacation. I jump up. "Off to the beach," I say, "and ice cream for lunch! Kathryn, you can squeeze lemons in your hair if you want. Andrew, you can go on George's boat if you wear a life jacket. But first, clean those rooms!"

Their groans fade as they run off. Pouring the last drops of lemony sweetness into my glass, I sit and look at my kitchen, the gathering place of my home. The smell of tomato sauce and onions from last night's lasagna lingers in the air; there's a sink full of soaking dishes I need to get to. I'll have to take down the curtains, splattered with yesterday's cake mix, and soak them as soon as I get the chance. The sandy floor needs attention, too, neglected in favor of the beach. On this morning I think of my mother. She'd love this kitchen of mine where we bump into each other, everyone with something to say. I take one last wipe with a cloth at a smudge on the refrigerator door, newly bared for this year's vast collection of notes, reminders, and successes and then I'm ready.

As we jump into the car and head to the ocean, I throw on my mirrored sunglasses. Kathryn rolls her eyes at me. She tells me they're not cool, but I catch her looking into the lenses to see her reflection. I'll miss them when they're in school. *You miss them when they're asleep*, I tell myself.

At the beach, Kathryn sits on "her" rock, holding half a lemon over her head, squeezing, hoping to coax out the last of the summer's blonde streaks. Andrew perfects his skim boarding. I'm surprised he doesn't fall; looking over his shoulder at me as he does to make sure I see it all. I am the luckiest woman in the world. I cannot stop living and loving in the nearness of my children.

Tomorrow, I'll hand out lunches, packed with attention to each request for more of this and less of that, one sandwich cut diagonally, the other right down the middle. No one in this house knows what deviled ham is; I hope they never will. Matthew will race out of the door on his way to work, saying he plans to buy his lunch today, and when he gets home he'll grumble about how much money he spent. I'll wish him a good day as I notice how tall he's become, how broad his shoulders are. Andrew will ask if the clock is still five minutes ahead and lead his sister to the bus. He's in his favorite shorts and I'll wipe the toothpaste from his lip. Kathryn uses a Lip Smacker quickly and tucks it in her jeans pocket. I'll hear *Bye, Mom; love you, Mom*, as they turn the corner. I stay in the kitchen for a while, listening to music and dancing a little.

In the evening, the room is alive again with stories of the day. The sounds of giggling and good-natured badgering drown out everything else. I'm pulled like a magnet, back and forth, from one face to the other, listening and loving the chaotic, charged energy; a dizzying frenzy of love and excitement. Do I have six children, or just the three I thought I had?

At times like this, when I am feeling blissfully tugged this way and that, I find some gentle pause. I watch the ordinary unfold. It's then I am reminded of what I learned from my mother, and in spite of my mother: that our love, hers and mine, was an unexpected treasure. Treasures aren't always emeralds and gems but discoveries. Contained in its own unique vessel, our love was earthy and porous. It was fragile. It held the feelings that went unmentioned, the kind that are raw, unrefined, painful, and yes, even divine. Many loves will teach lessons of their own but the love between a mother and a child is the first with a heartbeat of its' own. This love, this story of my mother and me, was a view into a kaleidoscope of thousands of surfaces, some shiny, some cracked.

I learned that love could feel like drowning, finding you gasping for air at the surface. There are times of drought and unquenchable thirst for all that never was. Love can be a struggle to be faithful to devotion when neglect and bitterness are sticking to the bottom of your soul. Love's yearnings flow over the brim, and the cupping of a small hand tries to catch the losses that seep through the myriad cracks.

I can see my mother in her silent, cold kitchen, wearing the dress of roses that bleed together. I can feel the heavy humidity she must have felt, like a storm bringing another round of fear, sadness and despair. The curve of her hips and the pout of her lip are reflected in my mirror, too, years later and unexpected. My girlish, faith-filled prayers were the dedicated patches and glue I hoped would hold us through the fissures of time and pain. And without clearly knowing it at the time, I lived it boldly for one simple reason. I just had to. There was no other way and I needed us. Because though often tattered and bruised, love survives. It's worth the effort.

The girl my mother was and the woman she became guides me, urging me to take this time in my life with my children; her voice in my ear now a warm oil of tenderness. I feel her spirit patting my bottom toward the best in life, close to the truth and the love that I know is there. She whispers to me, prays for me, centers me, and calls me back to all that is real. She brings me back to the Mother so that I know how to accept the gifts that are offered. She is as sure of my love for her as I am of her love for me and she knows joy for what I have. I pray that she sits in a heavenly place.

I return to my family, to their rousing conversation, and I inhale deeply. I breathe in the tranquility and the comfortable wisdom of love in this kitchen, in my home and in our hearts. Redemption and gratitude are mine and the air is full of the sweetness that follows a cleansing rain.

It is a scent I know well, my perfume of familiarity, now at peace. It is the scent of her.

ACKNOWLEDGMENTS

So very much gratitude is due.

First and foremost, thank you to eLectio Publishing and to Christopher Dixon for a visit on the phone during the first quiet day after bringing my youngest child to college. As I wondered what to do next with my life, this gentleman told me that he had spent time with my story. After so many years, this call, this "yes," was a gracious and exhilarating response not unlike a direct answer to a prayer. I thank Mr. Dixon, Jesse Greever (CEO), and the staff of eLectio Publishing for trusting that others might like to hold my work in their hands. I thank all for the work that makes that happen so that the sharing of a story could help others live some of my words into inspirations of their own.

Then, from the beginning: Heidi Connolly, my very first editor, a shepherd who sat beside me at my dining room table. She brought encouragement, pencils, erasers, skill and love to guide my handwritten pages. It was you who called me a writer and in the years that followed, I started to believe it. With love and gratitude, I thank Ann Tramonte for a very first reading and for her tears of recognition. You will always have a sister's love. How very fortunate I have been to have lived and grown up with the funniest two men in the world, my brothers, Jack and Brian. Laughter has been the glue that keeps us together. And to more friends and family: Tim and Lisa Smith, Mary Fitzgerald, Whitney Schmitt Laws, Wendy Ford, Bill Brokamp, Nancy Slonim Aronie and the Chilmark Writer's Workshop of summer 2011, Linda Regele, Peggy Anne Canty, Steve Huggard, Heidi Mallett, for all of your expressed wishes and interest, concerns, readings and so many kindnesses, I lovingly thank you. To Dr. Andrew X. Zhu, Dr. James Campbell Cusack, Michelle Knowles, N.P., Lanetta Giacona, N.P., and Jill Clarke Alexis, for healing and life. To the late Ginny McGrath, R.N., a light in my life, inspiring me to remember stories of nursing and the mission of healing. To Maureen DuCrest, my childhood friend, you have a heart of gold. I thank God for the blessings of my friend, Dr. David O'Hanley and the "just a thought" note. For my lily farmers, Carolyn and Dick Housman, I'm so grateful for the caring. Carolyn, my mentor, for life. Love and gratitude goes to Deacon Daniel Crimmins, my uncle, for always seeing the good in me. To Bernadette Donahue, a writer, too, I love you dear Aunt. To Matilda Butler and Kendra Bonnett, memoir coaches, for publishing my essays on life during recent years on WomensMemoirs.com: how talented, lovely and inspiring you have been. To John J. O'Leary and Joan O'Leary: I hope you're together in a heavenly embrace. Thank you for my life and so much love.

To Helen O'Leary, my aunt and friend, for always believing in me, for teaching me to reach toward things that bring life and for all of the humble ways in which you give love to all of God's children. You are my teacher.

To Nancy Jones Brokamp: my soul friend; for holding me up, giving me faith and for seeing the little girl in me. For the tears and the joys we have known and shared. You are my right arm.

To Brian, thank you for untold freedoms that have let me love and live in the ways I've needed to. For front row seats to James Taylor: unbelievable. For the years of climbing trees for bittersweet branches, just for me.

Finally, the greatest blessings of all: Matthew, my first, it is an honor to be your mother. I am so proud of your strength and I see into your generous soul. So much good is coming your way. Andrew, you are my holy listener, my sweet missionary, in whom I am well pleased. Write your heart out. Kathryn, my green-eyed baby, full of grace, you enliven my spirits with your dreams. I believe in you.

Made in the USA
Charleston, SC
18 November 2015